Burden of Faith

DEAN MAGDAL THOMPSON

© 2008 Dean Magdal Thompson
All Rights Reserved.

No part of this publication may be reproduced, stored in a retrieval system, or transmitted, in any form or by any means, electronic, mechanical, photocopying, recording, or otherwise, without the written permission of the author.

First published by Dog Ear Publishing
4010 W. 86th Street, Ste H
Indianapolis, IN 46268
www.dogearpublishing.net

dog ear
PUBLISHING

ISBN: 978-159858-609-1

This book is printed on acid-free paper.

Printed in the United States of America

Chapter 1

God was not in His heaven that warm summer night, as the freight train lurched up the grade toward the sleepy Texas town of Bandera. If He had been, surely He would have let Death sleep. Unfortunately, the staccato shock of couplings reaching their limit awoke Death.

Death was alone that night, which was usual for this backwater run, meandering west through San Antonio to nowhere in particular. Nocturnal travelers had long ago learned there was nothing gained, and everything to lose in the company of creatures such as Death.

Placing his tattooed shoulder against the frame, Death forced the heavy door open just as the lights of Bandera snaked into view. As the freight entered the town, clattering through one squalid neighborhood after another, Death waited patiently in the shadows nursing his bottle. Finally, taking a long last swig, he grabbed the doorframe and swung his powerful body out into the wind. Landing hard on loose gravel, Death fell cursing, onto the roadbed as the train rolled on unconcerned into the night.

The trip from Huntsville Prison to the park in Bandera had taken most of the day. As Death rose, checking the switchblade in his boot, food weighed heavily on his mind. Drawn by the prospect of a hot meal, Death shuffled off through the trees.

Not far enough away, Juan and Maria strolled through the park, as had countless lovers before them. As they walked arm in arm, Maria's thoughts returned to her eventful day, much of which they had managed to spend together. She remembered how she had struggled to be attentive in church and helpful during the midday meal, all the while keeping this most precious part of her life safely within her heart. There was, of course, the unfortunate necessity of lying about her intentions as she escaped to meet with her Juan. Maria disliked deceiving her parents. Nevertheless, she could do little else. She knew Juan would not be welcome in her life until she was old enough to marry, a point her parents had made abundantly clear. Fate, it seemed, had presented her with the classic lover's dilemma: rules she could not live with, concerning a man she could not live without.

Bandera's park ran along the Medina River between the rail line and the town. Although otherwise unremarkable, the park contained one extraordinary jewel. Nestled within it, lay a crescent shaped pond embracing a narrow passage, along which the two now walked.

Breaking out of the trees at the center of the isthmus, they stood for a moment transfixed, as swans glided gently across the water, leaving gossamer trails glistening in the moonlight. Entranced by Maria's radiance, Juan reached out to her and pulled her close.

Several quiet moments passed before the lovers continued toward the gazebo, its privacy beckoning to them from but a short distance away. Laughing at nothing in particular, they entered and fell into each other's arms—kissing passionately.

At first, Maria squirmed playfully as Juan unbuttoned her blouse to fondle her breasts. But soon, Maria settled back against him, slowly becoming aware of the warmth from his erection swelling between them. Maria smiled and raised her lips to kiss Juan. She was proud to be able to create such passion in their love. She knew that soon they would be married in the church, and then she would be free to give herself to him, accepting from him that which she now so desperately desired.

Gently, Juan laid Maria down on the bench and pressed his body to hers. As they clung to each other, Juan's hand moved from Maria's breast and crossed her skirt, to caress her pubic mound. Her passion growing, Maria moaned softly and instinctively relaxed her thighs. A few moments later, however, Maria once again began her now familiar struggle. "Baby no, we can't!" she murmured, taking Juan's hand from the place that only moments before had welcomed his touch.

Each time it was like this…

Each time, their first innocent brush of lips invariably led to more insistent expressions of their desire, and to the dream. It was Maria's dream, and each time it came, she would struggle sadly back through the enveloping veil of her passion, back through the remnants of her resolve, back from the abyss. For her dream was of a child—their child. However, it was not to be conceived at this time or in this place.

Pushing Juan away, Maria's heart cried at the rejection in his eyes. Softening, she melted once again into his arms and tenderly placed her hand on his manhood.

"Come Juanito; let me do this for you." Slowly at first, Maria moved with Juan in the now familiar rhythm they shared, until his body arched in completion.

His fevered passion spent, Maria held Juan in her arms and dreamed, as lovers will about their future. First, of course, would be the wedding, but then as soon as possible, would come the child.

"Juanito, that shall be his name."

"No," Juan countered. "I think it should be Chuy. Chuy's a *muy macho* name—befitting my son."

"I am *not* gonna name our child Chuy. You know how I feel about that man. You're such an asshole! Why are you always slamming me this way?"

"Because my little *Señorita*, you're so easy."

"Don't call me easy," Maria growled. "I know what that means."

"Okay then, if it's a girl, we shall call her Maria."

"I don't especially like that either, but if it'll make you happy…"

"*You* make me happy," Juan whispered, taking Maria in his arms, once again molding her body to his.

Time stood still for a few moments, but only a few. Too soon, the lovers rose and once again stepped out under the stars. As Maria raised her eyes to gaze upon her love, she felt a sudden chill. Moving closer to Juan, she neither heard nor saw the blow that lifted her off her feet and drove her face-first onto the path. The massive two-fisted hammer-like blow struck Maria between the shoulder blades—taking her breath away. As she fell, the impact of her teeth on the rough surface of the path cruelly lacerated her cheek. Confused and spitting blood, Maria tried to rise, but her legs no longer obeyed. She opened her eyes, but a violet mist obscured her view.

Unable to make sense of what was happening to her, Maria remained unaware of the life-and-death struggle, taking place just inches away. Suddenly, terror insinuated itself into her consciousness as a powerful presence grasped her from above, violently shook her, then cast her down. With the stench of whisky and old sweat enveloping her, Maria was forced to endure Death's touch. As she knelt, trembling, the sudden flash of a naked blade rekindled the panic within her. In desperation, she struggled to her feet and ran. Once again, however, Death overtook her and hurled her to the ground.

Maria began to cry as the sound of her clothing being cut from her body hammered its reality home to her. Indeed, it was but a moment before she felt the first painful thrust as Death attempted to pierce her innocence.

"Please *Señor*, stop!" Maria pleaded, twisting her hips to evade his attack. "Please, don't do this!"

Death grabbed her pubic hair and held her in place. Resigned to her fate, Maria awaited the inevitable penetration. Suddenly, an unspeakable horror overwhelmed her, as Death, thrust his knife into her vagina and savagely cut her. With searing pain coursing through her body, Maria screamed in tortured agony and collapsed.

Chapter 2

As if through a haze, Maria watched the lights flash by. There were sounds too, confusing sounds…and voices, voices she could not recognize. But most of all there was pain, more pain than she had ever known. She tried to find the pain, to soothe it, to make it go away, but unseen hands prevented her touch.

Finally, as if her tears had washed them away, the pain subsided, the flashing lights dimmed, and the voices no longer spoke to her.

"Have you seen our latest?"

"You mean the young girl they flew in from Bandera?"

"Yeah, that's the one. Bandera-Medical thought she was just another beat up rape victim until they saw all the blood."

"Thank God they realized she was out of their league in time to AirLife her here."

"What is she, 17 maybe 18? Jesus!"

"Too young to have her life destroyed like this, that's for sure."

"Did you see her face? You can tell she was beautiful, but now…"

"It's not just her face that's been ruined."

"With all that damage, it's a miracle she didn't die before they found her."

"You're not kidding; the doctors don't have a clue how she survived."

"You know he cut her."

"Why'd he have to do that, couldn't he penetrate her?"

"They say he not only cut her hymen, the vicious bastard went inside and sliced her all the way to the uterus."

"What kind of monster would do something like that to a child?"

"He must have known she could never have children after that."

"Pray to God she doesn't even try. Just getting pregnant could kill her."

"I'm sorry, but it sure sounds like some kind of revenge thing to me."

"That's ridiculous. What on earth could the child have done to deserve something like this?"

"Nothing, it's just insane."

"Do they think it was a boyfriend or someone like that?"

"No, haven't you heard? I understand they found her boyfriend's body at the scene. Apparently, he died trying to protect her. Whoever attacked them was just too powerful I guess."

"It had to be some rotten bastard passing through. I hope they find him and put him away forever."

"Not much chance of that. Bandera's full of transients, what with the trains coming through at all hours, and the highway."

"You're right, that son-of-a-bitch's probably halfway to Hell by now."

Time had lost its meaning for Maria as she vaguely became aware of the rain falling against her window. Confused and afraid, she tried to rise, but successive waves of intense pain forced her back.

"Lie still. Don't try to move."

"What's happened to me, where…where am I?" Maria asked the nurse.

"You're in San Antonio at the Methodist Hospital. You've had a bad time, but you're safe now."

"I hurt so bad…down there," Maria said, lifting the edge of her blanket.

"Don't, Sweetie," the nurse said, gently removing her hand. "There's really nothing to see."

"Do you remember anything about the attack, about last evening, I mean?"

"No, I don't think…Oh God, where's my Juanito? Is he all right?"

Maria again tried to rise. "Please, tell me where he is. Please!"

"Shush now, Child. It won't do any good to upset yourself. I'll try to find out about your friend, I promise. But now you must try to rest."

Another week passed before Maria learned that her beloved Juan had died during the attack, but she *never* learned of the traces of sperm found within her.

Maria knocked and entered the doctor's office; its opulence surprised her. She had never seen anything like it in Bandera, and it made her *very* uncomfortable. She was increasingly aware of how expensive her treatment had been, and wondered how much of it was reflected in the room where she now stood. Maria was certain insurance had helped, but sensed her parents' modest resources were being devastated as well. Knowing this, Maria had vowed to do whatever she could to shorten her stay. When asked how she felt, Maria's response, even in pain, was invariably "fine." Without complaint, she withstood every therapeutic exercise, swallowed every disgusting pill, and, although nausea often followed, even struggled through her meals. Therefore, with a silent resolve never to set foot in the hospital again, Maria settled into her expensive chair and listened to the doctor, for what she hoped would be the very last time.

"I know you're anxious to get home," the doctor began, "so I won't keep you any longer than necessary. However, it's important that we have this talk before you go. There are a few issues we need to discuss, but before we get to them, the staff," he motioned to the nurse who had entered with her, "and I want you to know how pleased we are with your progress."

"Thank you," Maria said, attempting a smile.

The doctor nodded and glanced at his notes. "Although you're obviously well enough to go home, you're not completely healed, so you'll need to take it easy for a while. In addition, I'm putting you on a special regimen to help with your recovery. One of the medications I want you to take will suppress your periods. Your system is far too fragile to handle the bleeding of menses."

Is he kidding, she wondered. Seems like bleeding's all I've done lately.

"I'm also giving you a rather powerful prescription to manage the pain, at least for the next few weeks. While you're taking the pills, you may experience some mild abdominal discomfort…nausea, especially in the morning."

More pills, Maria frowned. As if there haven't been enough already.

Seeming to notice her concern, the doctor quickly added, "We've actually had you on this program for some time now, so we know you'll do fine."

Except for feeling like crap, she thought.

"As far as the healing process goes, you can expect some minor pain and swelling, at least for the next few months."

Jesus, I don't like the sound of this.

"And finally, your hormonal imbalance will undoubtedly result in an occasional dream, probably accompanied by some fairly intense emotions."

Oh, God, not more dreams!

"Some of the episodes may be quite vivid—especially if they relate to your attack. Nevertheless, I think we can reasonably expect them to subside as soon as you're off the menses suppression drugs. Should they persist, however, I want you to come back in and we'll have you visit with one of our counselors."

Not in this lifetime, she thought, furtively glancing at the nurse beside her, and not unless things get a hell of a lot worse than they already are.

"When you get home, I want you to visit the medical center in Bandera and schedule your follow-up exams. Are you familiar with the facility?"

"Yes, my Aunt Virginia's a nurse there."

"Wonderful, I'll forward your records directly to her.

I know this all sounds new to you, Maria. Do you have any questions?"

"No, I don't think so," she answered softly.

The doctor paused, as if deciding the best way to proceed.

Maria noticed...

"There's one last very important issue we need to discuss—pregnancy. It's vitally important that you not become pregnant during your recovery."

Pregnant? I don't...I don't understand. What's he saying?

With painful emotions flooding her senses, Maria barely noticed the nurse take her hand.

"In fact," he continued, "you must take appropriate precautions from now on. Were you to try to carry a baby to term, you would almost certainly abort. Should that happen, and you're unable to get to a hospital, you could conceivably bleed to death. Even if you were able to carry the baby full term, there's no certainty that you, or the baby would survive the delivery."

Oh God, No! Maria's eyes began to tear as the doctor's words seared into her heart.

"I can't have children...ever?" The nurse's grasp tightened on her hand. "My God! You...you can't mean that, you just *can't!*"

"I'm sorry, Maria. I wish something could be done, some hope we could offer, but the risks are just too great."

"What about my parents? Oh God, how'm I ever gonna tell them they won't have grandchildren? This can't be happening!"

"Would you like me to talk with your parents?" the doctor offered. "Surely, they'll understand."

"*Understand?*" Maria yanked her hand free and stormed toward the door. "You're the one who doesn't understand, Doctor!"

Chapter 3

June 7: Dear Diary
    Thank God, I'm finally home! I thought they'd never let me out of that freaking hospital. I don't know where to begin. My face is totally destroyed and I hurt all the time. I've so many stitches; I look like a patchwork quilt. Whenever my mouth moves the wrong way, something gets pushed or pulled and I start to bleed. Hopefully, it's just a matter of time till everything heals.

June 14: Dear Diary
    God, I wish I'd get over this nausea! I puke every time I take those damn pills, and when I throw up, it feels like his knife is still inside me. And another thing. Every relative in South Texas has been parading through here wanting to hug me and I just can't do that yet.

June 30: Dear Diary
> These damn dreams are becoming a major problem. My brain keeps dragging me back through the rape in disgusting detail. The worst is, I've begun to remember things I'd somehow suppressed. It's so vivid; I can almost feel that bastard forcing himself into me, the pain of his repeated thrusting—and his climax. I keep thinking his semen is somehow mixed in with my blood and he's part of me now.

Each night, somewhere between dusk and dawn, Maria would once again fall painfully onto the path. Each night, Juan would be there, staring back through unseeing eyes. Each night, she would crawl the short distance between them and reach out to touch him. Each night she would once again realize her Juan was dead. Each night Maria would awaken with a start, and each morning she would cry.

July 22: Dear Diary
> Thank God, my screwed up cheek's finally healed. Unfortunately, I'm gonna look like hammered shit the rest of my life. At least the puking's stopped and I can eat again. Now if only the bills would stop as well. It's been almost three months and I really need to get a job. I don't know who'll hire me though with my face all fucked up.

Maria watched helplessly as her family's dreams stripped away—layer by layer. Her father had worked his entire life to provide a decent living for the family. Hard work, however, was no match for the medical bills he now faced. Unable to cope with both an injured daughter and looming financial ruin, he had begun to drink.

Maria's mother dealt with her own special Hell. It seemed that God had finally gotten around to punishing her for not having a second child. They had intended to have several children, but Maria's birth had been extremely difficult. The memory of her unrelenting pain never again allowed her to consent to her husband's desire for another child—and now it was too late. Time, it seemed, had robbed her of the ability to conceive. Thus, she spent much of each day contemplating her sin.

> August 5: Dear Diary
> I feel okay, but I've noticed a scary change in my emotions. Where I used to run and greet everyone, now I hesitate and hang back. It makes me angry knowing another precious part of my life's been taken from me.
> That's about it I guess, except I'm going to Imelda's again in the morning. Maybe she can cheer me up.

Imelda was Maria's dearest friend from high school, an institution she no longer wished to attend—for she knew her scars would not be easily tolerated. Maria also knew it would be different with Imelda. She was special, as was their relationship. When Maria hurt, Imelda cried. When Imelda cried, Maria hurt. It had been that way since they were children together, not so many years before.

Throughout their visit, Maria had dreaded the question she knew, would eventually be asked. It had poisoned their conversation that morning like an infected cyst, until…Here it comes, she thought, as Imelda settled back, her stare, boring deep into Maria's eyes.

"Do you think you'll ever find a love to replace Juan?"

"I don't think so. I haven't told anyone, but I can't even stand my own father's touch, let alone that of another man. Even when I try to remember how it was with Juan, when I felt such passion, now it's…different."

"What do you mean 'different'?"

"I feel so empty, almost dead inside. It's like hugging without being held. The only passion I feel in my heart now, is fear."

"What about your family? How are they taking it?"

"They seem to understand. Most of them just leave me alone. Except for Chuy of course, he never changes. We used to have this private joke. Whenever he'd see me, he'd whisper in my ear, 'Consider yourself hugged,' and I'd say, 'Consider yourself hugged back.' Well, last week he whispered, 'Consider yourself kissed,' and without thinking, I shot back, 'Consider yourself dead.' It was sad, we didn't know whether to laugh or cry."

"Sometimes," Maria sighed, "it feels like I've nothing left to live for. Maybe it would've been better if I'd just died along with Juan."

"Don't say that!" Imelda lunged forward in her chair. "It'll be all right, you'll see."

"No, Imelda?" Maria snapped. "I *don't* see."

Now I'm *really* getting worried, Imelda thought, as Maria left for home. Oh, I hope she doesn't do anything stupid.

Chapter 4

Women are not stupid…
women have always known that there was a life there.
—Faye Wattleton, then President of Planned Parenthood

Maria was scared!

Despite having been off the dreaded pills for over a month, she still experienced their characteristic side effects. She also had not had a normal period, and did not expect to for at least another month, although there *had* been some significant spotting. In addition, she continued to feel an occasional flutter in her belly. The straw that broke the proverbial camel's back, however, was the realization that her abdominal swelling, which lessened for a time, had returned with a vengeance. Remembering her vow, never to set foot in San Antonio's hospital again, Maria instead turned to her Aunt Virginia for help.

As Virginia listened, an uncomfortable suspicion crept into her mind. Disturbing, and in Maria's case, supposedly impossible, and yet, she appeared to be recovering well. Her pain was gone and her normal strength seemed to have returned. There were still some lingering emotional issues, but overall...So what else could it be? The answer was, of course, that it couldn't be anything else. Maria must be pregnant, and *that* was not a good thing!

My God, Virginia thought. Her treatment's been masking the pregnancy.

At first, they discussed the possibility in a calm, mature manner—of how the medication might still be at fault. If that were the case, any informal tests Virginia could do at home would also be suspect, so a blood test at the clinic was required. She made a mental note to schedule one for the next day. I might as well schedule a counseling session too, she thought. Maria may need it.

"Jesus!" Maria gasped, suddenly remembering the doctor's final warning, that a pregnancy could kill her *and* the baby. "Oh Jesus!" she repeated, as strange feelings began to kick in, emotions she had never experienced before. There was fear of course, but something more, something protective, almost...maternal.

Maria thanked her aunt, promised to meet her at the clinic early the next morning, then quickly left—heading straight for Bandera's Pharmacy. Although in many ways Maria was naïve, she did know about home pregnancy tests. She had even tried one once with Imelda on a lark. Nothing happened, of course, although Imelda's did give them a bit of a scare, as the indicator flipped between life and death.

Pausing but a moment to wave to her parents as she arrived home, Maria ran for the bathroom. Alone at last, she slipped out of her panties and dutifully hovered over the strip to pee.

Neither prayers nor luck was enough to evade the result she already knew within her heart. Death, it seemed, had changed her more profoundly that fateful night than she would ever have imagined.

It's true. I'm gonna have a baby, she thought. My God, I'm gonna have a baby...No, I *am* having a baby. It's in me now...alive in me right now...and like my Juanito, *it's gonna die!*

Maria trembled and leaned forward on the toilet as reality came crashing in on her. *How'd the doctor put it? If you get pregnant, the baby might abort at any moment. If you're unable to get to a hospital, you could bleed to death.*

Somehow, the thought of getting pregnant, let alone dying, had always seemed like a dream to Maria, something that *could* happen, but never really would.

If it happens in Bandera, I'll be fine, she thought, but my baby will die...My baby will die, alone!

A crushing sadness came over her, sadness she did not fully understand. In an instant, however, she knew what she had to do.

My baby must not die alone. Please, God, help me!

No one seemed to notice, and certainly, no one cared as the slight girl-of-a-woman boarded the bus to Laredo later that evening.

It was early morning as Maria crossed the border into Mexico, but she knew the *Pharmacia* would already be open. She also knew where to find it, thanks to Imelda.

Upon entering the store, Maria waited patiently for the pharmacist to finish with his other customers before she discreetly approached. The pharmacist was accustomed to receiving requests of a delicate or embarrassing nature, but Maria's was a bit more than he possibly expected.

"I was told you could help me," she said, "with—some kind of pill, to…to end my pregnancy."

The elderly pharmacist frowned. "Who told you I could, or even would do such a thing?"

Maria leaned forward and whispered, "Your niece in Bandera."

The pharmacist studied Maria for a long moment, and then motioned for her to follow him into his office. As she sat down, Maria noted the comfortably worn chair was much more to her liking than the doctor's had been.

"Why do you wish to rid yourself of this baby so easily?" the pharmacist asked.

"It's not easy!" she said smarting. "I have no choice."

Once again, the pharmacist frowned. "There are always choices, child. If you want my help, you're going to have to trust me. Now, what's going on?"

"The baby is from a rape," she continued slowly. "He…he hurt me."

"What do you mean?"

"I can't have this baby, any baby. If I don't do this, the doctors say we'll both die."

Incredulous, the pharmacist asked, "Is this true?"

"*Sí*, there's no other way for me."

The pharmacist reached out and touched Maria's chin, gently turning her disfigured cheek toward the light. "He did this to you as well?"

Slowly lowering her eyes, Maria nodded.

"Bastard," the pharmacist muttered as he wearily rose and left the office. "*Un momento, por favor.*"

In the requested moment, he returned, wordlessly handing Maria a small plastic container. The pharmacist waved her off when she reached for her purse to pay for the pill. "Things such as this are not purchased with money…as you shall see."

The pharmacist took Maria's hand as she stood to leave. "You must be strong child, stronger than you've ever been. Take God with you also, for without Him, you'll surely fail and pay a terrible price."

Maria leaned forward once again, placing a kiss on the pharmacist's cheek. "*Gracias, Señor*," she said, fighting back a tear.

On their way out, the pharmacist paused to retrieve an information pamphlet about the pill, but as he turned to give it to Maria, she was gone.

As she entered her motel room, Maria wondered if the kindly old pharmacist would ever realize she'd deceived him. If so, she hoped he would understand—she just couldn't let her baby die alone. Maria toyed with the thought for a moment, and then put it out of her mind. There were too many other things to do, before…

She had planned to write a short note to her parents and Aunt Virginia, explaining why she had done, what she was about to do. But as she wrote, she found it more comforting just to tell them she loved them.

She also made a list of her material treasures and who should receive them. As she went about these tasks, Maria would occasionally place her hand over the spot where she imagined her baby lay sleeping. She felt unusually calm, mysteriously content.

Maria ignored the pill as long as possible. She had placed it by her chair and there it remained, lying lightly on the table, yet heavily on her mind. All day long, there had been nothing but the clock and the pill. The clock's ticking representing life, the pill's silence representing death—Maria's death and that of her baby.

In the evening, as the time grew near, she sat down in front of the pill. Taking a deep breath, Maria extended a finger to touch it. Slowly she rolled and turned it, seeking the source of its malevolence.

The room grew dark. Maria began to speak, but not to the pill. She whispered, instead, as a mother to her baby. Softly, she spoke of her love and the special places within her heart. She told her baby of her dreams and of her beloved Juan. Finally, she told her baby about the pill, of how it would allow them to be together always, and of how she had asked God to shield her baby from its pain.

It was time...

Trembling now, Maria reached for the pill and placed it in her mouth.

It was time...

The crushing pain awoke Maria, driving her knees into her chest. She tried to scream through jaws clamped shut by waves of nausea. Unable to rise, she slid painfully to the floor and struggled toward the bathroom. The cold ceramic tile chilled Maria through her wet gown as the pungent odor of urine enveloped her. Instinctively, she held her hand over her vagina as she felt the baby sliding through her. Unable to pull herself onto the toilet, Maria collapsed to the floor as a crimson pool slowly expanded around her.

Her baby was gone.

Nurse Virginia Galvan had just finished dressing for work when the phone rang—as expected. It had been a bad night. Virginia had managed little more than an occasional catnap since discovering Maria had fled. Now, with dread squeezing her heart in its icy grip, she held little hope today would be any better. Her fear gave way to relief, however, as she realized it was Maria on the line, then to concern as she heard her fragile voice, and finally to tears as she learned what her dear Maria had done.

Maria had actually said very little, only that she was in Nuevo Laredo and was too weak to make the trip home—and that her baby was gone. She begged her aunt not to tell her parents, in order to spare them additional pain. Then promising to explain further, when Virginia arrived, Maria abruptly hung up the phone.

Wiping a tear, Virginia turned her car onto the highway and headed for the border.

What Maria could not reveal on the long dusty trip back to Bandera, were her feelings when she awoke—alive and alone—to discover that what had only hours before been her baby, was now nothing more than the bloody mess she lay in. A mess *she* would have to clean.

Chapter 5

What was the lowest moment [of your life]?

*You know, I guess, I hate to talk about this on the air,
but having an abortion.*

*At the time I was just young and dumb,
I didn't really want to have a baby then.
It was the wrong thing to do and I really didn't understand that till later.*

That was very very painful, that was probably the worst.

—Ellen Burstyn - LifeSiteNews.com, 2007

Maria felt her life was over.
    Since returning from Laredo, she had found little comfort other than to sit each day feeding birds from her window. Her nights were no better, as her conscience continued to assail her. Every night she would once again fall painfully onto the path and discover her beloved Juan was dead. Now, however, a child would be standing over him, crying out in desperation. The anguished child in her dreams profoundly wounded Maria. Even with Imelda's loving care, she remained vulnerable to the relentless depression grinding her down. Finally, unable to bear her

burden any longer, she decided to go where she had dreaded to go and do what she had dreaded to do. Maria would place her sins before God.

Maria entered the confessional and crossed herself.

"Forgive me Father for I have sinned. It's been six months since my last confession."

"Why have you waited so long, my child?" the priest asked.

"My sin is so terrible that…that I felt even God might not forgive me."

"That's not for you to decide, now is it?"

"No, Father."

"Tell me then, what burdens you so?"

"I was raped six months ago."

"I'm sorry. Did you do anything to cause this sin?"

"I don't think so. He was a stranger."

"I see. Is there anything else you wish to tell me?"

"Yes, Father. I became pregnant from the sin."

"What has become of your baby?"

"It…it's gone."

"What do you mean 'gone'?"

"I…I took a pill. The baby was—"

"A pill? You mean an abortion pill?"

"Yes, Father."

"Oh my child, what've you done?"

"The baby was of the sin, Father! It was not Juan's."

"Juan is your husband?"

"No, Father, Juan was my life. He died trying to protect me from the rapist."

"I see," the priest said sadly.

"Father, please help me. I hurt so bad, inside."

"Is there anything else?" the priest asked.

"No, Father."

"Tell me then. Why have you come to me?" his tone hardening.

"I wanted to confess, to be clean again, to—"

"You wanted to *feel* better."

"Yes, Father."

"The rape was not your fault my child," the priest began, "you needn't ask God's forgiveness for that. Your baby, however, is another matter."

"But...but the baby was of the sin," Maria repeated.

"*Of* a sin and *being* a sin are two very different things. While the Church recognizes rape as a sin, a child conceived in rape is just as innocent, just as precious as any other child. In deciding to abort...to kill your baby, you have committed a sin more grievous than that of the rapist."

"But the baby...I had no choice," she pleaded.

"No, my child. May God forgive you, for you have sacrificed an innocent."

The priest continued to speak as Maria burst from the confessional and ran, crying, out into the night.

The end was very near for Maria. Her seemingly infinite capacity for life had finally ebbed away and the only chance for redemption, denied her. Tonight would see the end of her pain—the last of her tears.

Maria was taking no chances at leaving a mess like the one in Mexico. A shower curtain lay over her bed and a plastic-lined wastebasket stood beside it—just in case. She had thought about wearing her new skirt and blouse, but hoped Imelda would make better use of them. In the end, she decided to wear only the matching bra and panties she had purchased in anticipation of her honeymoon with Juan. Maria hoped she would arrive in heaven wearing the same garments she died in, and thought Juan would be pleased.

She waited quietly in her room until her parents were asleep before searching for her father's whisky bottle, which did not take much of an effort to find.

Back in her room, Maria retrieved her own hidden cache of pills, left over from her recovery. She had not taken them earlier because of the severe nausea they caused. Now they would serve a new, more sinister purpose. Maria placed a few pills in her mouth and attempted to wash them down with whiskey. It did not go well. Steeling her nerves, she repeated the process several more times until all the pills were gone. She was preparing herself for what was to come. The whisky would provide the courage; the pills would prevent the pain.

Slowly, Maria picked up the razor and lay back on the bed waiting for the lethal combination to kick in; it did not take long. As she felt the numbness spreading within her, she lifted the razor and slashed at her wrist.

With the reality of what she had just done screaming for her attention, she became distracted instead by a dream. As she watched the pictures her emotions drew across her mind, the hand holding the razor slowly dropped to her side.

Maria was drunk, and, thanks to the pills, she was once again about to be very sick.

Bolting suddenly upright, Maria raised her head just in time to project the toxic mixture of whisky and pills across the room.

"Damn!" she exclaimed.

She sat stunned, staring into space for several moments before looking down at her wrist and realizing she had botched another job.

"Damn!" she repeated. "What's going on?"

Maria wiped the residual blood from her wrist before walking unsteadily to her closet for jeans and blouse. She dressed quickly and left the house—heading back to the church.

Bandera was still asleep as Maria pushed open the church door and quietly slipped inside. The lights had been extinguished hours before and the sun had not yet replaced them, so the only illumination came from candles drowning in ancient pools of wax upon the altar.

Maria was shaking. But this, it seemed, was how God would want her: lost, scared and vulnerable. His task would be easier this way—His blessings more profound.

So it was for Maria. She had lost her love and seemingly her capacity for love. She had lost her baby and her ability to conceive. She had lost every reason to live, yet she lived still—and she wanted to know why.

Walking slowly and deliberately toward the altar, Maria's eyes never left the crucifix hanging on high. Emotions exploded within her at every step—for she had come to talk with her God. She placed her hands on the altar and dropped slowly to her knees. There she knelt, holding on to God as if there were nowhere else to go.

Her tears came before her appeal. Her chin trembled, and so too did her voice as she pleaded with her God.

"Why won't you let me die? Why won't you accept me? WHY?"

Her tears were heavier now, as seemed her burden. The last of her strength finally gone, the altar slipped from her grasp as she collapsed to the floor. No longer able to rise, she laid her scarred cheek against the cool tile, now wet with her tears, closed her eyes and gave herself up to God.

In the beginning, there was nothing, merely emptiness, cold, dark...and deadly. The bitter gloom swirling about Maria, bathed her in a gray hopeless despair, and so she slept. In time, however, the vivid hues of faith weaved themselves back into her dreams, softening her furrowed brow, relaxing her angry fists. Then, as the warmth of God's love entered her, healing her, making all things new, she awakened in the light.

Grace thus came to Maria as she slept, infusing within her a peace transcending all sin.

Maria was...reborn!

Suitcase in hand, Maria stopped by the clinic. She had come to tell Virginia goodbye and to thank her for everything she had done. Her aunt's initial smile quickly evaporated, however, as she noticed the bandage across Maria's wrist. Not wanting Virginia to worry unnecessarily, Maria assured her it was only a scratch and that everything was fine.

Maria told her aunt she had decided to move to San Antonio. "There are too many ghosts for me here in Bandera. Besides," she explained, "I feel like God wants me there."

"What do you mean, 'God wants you there'?" Virginia asked.

"I see now that all these terrible things that have happened weren't really about me. I think it was just God preparing me, sorta like He'd shape a tool, for something important. I don't know what it is yet, but I'm sure God will reveal it to me in His own good time."

"But why would God work in such a violent way?" Virginia asked.

"I know it's hard to accept, but I think He wanted me to feel…no, *to believe*, that whatever happens to me, no matter how terrible, He'll be with me and protect me—because I'm important, somehow a part of His plan. It's like in the Bible. How's it go? '*For I know the plans I have for you…plans to prosper you and not to harm you, plans to give you hope and a future.*' So, even though I might not understand, He's determined that I live, because He needs me."

"You're scaring me again, child," Virginia said with a frown. "Do me one favor. Promise me you won't take any unnecessary chances just because you think your butt's made of steel."

Maria smiled. "Okay I promise," she said, walking through the door in search of a new life.

Chapter 6

The promise of a new life attracted Katherine Reed to San Antonio as well. Katherine, or Kat, as she preferred, was alone in the world, and now, a week before Christmas, she felt it intensely. Orphaned at birth, she had lived with her grandparents in Enid, Oklahoma for as much of her life as she could remember. But, "in the fullness of time," they, too, had passed. Confronted with the reality of having to look after herself, Kat entered the University of Tulsa, from which, she emerged some four years later with a degree in economics and a job offer from the Southwestern Life Insurance Company. Kat's transition from Enid to San Antonio had been rocky at best. Although Enid was not rural by any reasonable measure, it *was* remote enough to have avoided the ethnic storms, proclaiming San Antonio their home. The comfort of life-long relationships had ill-prepared Kat for her transfer to the far side of the moon. Her inability to assimilate within the Hispanic community saddened her profoundly. Faced with little else, Kat had immersed herself in her work.

It was late in the evening of yet another long day at Southwestern Life, when Kat paused at her keyboard to gaze at her grandparents' picture. She sighed deeply, leaned back in her chair and stretched. As she did, she vaguely became aware of the muted sounds of music and laughter coming from somewhere down the hall. Listening for a moment, she concluded that for some, the holiday season had officially begun. Kat closed her eyes, freeing her weary mind to visualize the happy scene. Unfortunately, this quickly led to the usual unpleasant comparison with her current plight. Her motivation for work gone, Kat checked the time and decided to leave the rest for another day.

As if anyone would notice, or care.

Kat picked up her purse, turned the lights off in her cube, and slowly headed for the exit.

As she approached the elevator, however, the music's heavy beat reached out to her. While pushing the elevator button with one hand, she subconsciously kept time against her thigh with the other.

There really isn't any reason to rush home she thought, contemplating her options. It's not as if anyone was waiting…besides the cat, that is.

Finally, rationalizing what she had already decided to do, Kat uttered, "Sorry, Puddy Tat," and continued down the hall.

Hoping to escape detection, she stood for a few moments in the shadows before slipping through the open door. Wandering discreetly between the food and the bar, Kat recognized several of her coworkers. It seemed she was not the only one drawn to the music's compelling beat.

Nevertheless, her mood and the music eventually succumbed to the lateness of the hour, and her need to continue on home. As she rose to leave, however, a Latino voice, dripping with sensuality reached out and seduced her resolve. Entranced as a moth to a flame, Kat snaked her way through the crowd to discover its hallowed source. Entering the innermost ring of her new universe, she watched as Tio-the-spider, spun his erotic web around the room.

Tio's back was to Kat as he worked his magic, enabling her to watch every move and listen to his every word without fear of detection. It was quite a show, and Kat enjoyed it immensely—until Tio turned around. He paused for but a moment, only long enough to capture her within his eyes and to create a spell to last a thousand years, then he turned away.

Kat found it difficult to stand and almost impossible to move, but she had to, for her nipples were becoming hard as rocks. Self-consciously pulling her scarf down to cover her breasts, Kat unsteadily walked away.

The party was held in a room with floor-to-ceiling walls of glass, providing a fantastic view of the city at night. Slipping onto a window seat, Kat turned her body to watch, as the vibrant scene pulsated below. Moments later and deep in thought, she became aware of a warm breath blowing over her hair. Startled, she turned to find Tio's smile filling her eyes and his voice—*that glorious voice*—whispering softly in her ear. Her world stopped, and he, God help her, obviously knew it. Somehow, she managed to talk with him, to drink with him, to even dance once, or was it twice with him? Kat was not sure. In fact, she was not sure of anything except she was in serious trouble—and did not care.

Maybe it was the heat in the room or just the heat in Kat, but when Tio offered to take her to the roof for some air, she quickly agreed. Although dimly lit at that hour, an abundance of moonlight and stars illuminated their path as they walked out onto the roof. The sensual breeze flowing over her fevered body reawakened Kat to Tio's closeness and reminded her once again to pull her scarf down across her breasts. As they continued walking, talking and laughing at nothing in particular, Kat began to feel the chill in the cool night air. Stepping behind a retaining wall to escape the breeze, Tio took Kat in his arms and gently rubbed her back to fend off the cold.

Intensely aware of Tio's passion, she found herself responding to the warmth of his body…the heat of his touch. Tilting her head forward, she slid her arms around his neck and nuzzled him. Tio's lips softly brushed her cheek, then the nape of her neck and then teasingly, moved away. Kat leaned back against the retaining wall and pouted, feigning disappointment. Tio smiled, then moved his hand to the back of her neck and pulled her now, playfully resisting lips to his.

Frozen in time and space, they kissed, and then kissed again with a passion and intensity matching their mutual need. As Tio greedily probed Kat's mouth with his tongue, he raised his hand to her breast, painting circles around her now fully erect nipple with his thumb. Around and around he went, each revolution sending its sensuous electricity straight to Kat's well-lubricated soul.

Tio cupped his hands under her bottom, pulling her groin against his hard and hungry sex. Trembling in her desire, Kat wantonly tipped her pelvis to meet him as he slid her pubic mound slowly up and down his swollen manhood. Kat's legs deserted her. If not for the pressure of Tio's body pinning her to the wall, she would have fallen as the first climax exploded within her. Kat's body arched reflexively. Tio pulled her lips to his, once again thrusting his tongue into her. All resistance gone, she sucked him hungrily.

Kat's mission in life was now clear. Tio's lust would totally define her reason for being. She would give herself to him, fully and without reservation, in any and every way he desired. When Tio kissed her neck, Kat lifted her scarf for him. When his lips moved lower, Kat stripped off her blouse for him. When he desired her breasts, Kat quickly unsnapped her bra and fed them to him—nothing was denied him.

As Tio knelt, continuing his carnal journey of exploration, Kat felt the heat of his hands as they stroked her thighs. Pausing but a moment, they inched upward. Sensing his intent, Kat lifted her skirt and held it at her waist, shamelessly exposing the very essence of her being to Tio's hot breath. As he returned to her arms, she felt the heat from his unsheathed penis against her leg. Unable to control her passion, Kat reached down to grasp him, to pull him within her, when, suddenly, she felt a quick, sharp stab as Tio impaled her.

Kat screamed…

This time, however, her cry was cut short by the scarf being tightened around her throat. Desperate for air, she raised her hand to loosen the scarf as climatic spasm after spasm surged through her. That was the last thing Kat remembered as she slipped into unconsciousness.

A gentle breeze caressed Kat as she awoke. Opening her eyes, she saw that dawn was just beginning. Although she knew where she was and knew what she had done, she was not quite sure what Tio had done to her, and, more importantly, why? She tried to move, but winced at the pain her action caused.

"Girl, you've really done it this time," she sighed, realizing she was more naked than not. Reaching to hook her bra, Kat felt Tio's dried semen on her exposed breasts. Embarrassed, she stood to retrieve her shoes and purse. As she adjusted her blouse, Kat discovered her scarf, still tightly knotted around her throat. Puzzled, she removed it, and then walked slowly across the roof and through the access door.

Kat entered her apartment and paused, the scarf still clutched in her hand. Turning to study her reflection in the hall mirror, she saw the fiery red bruises at her throat. Sadness swept through her and she began to cry.

Later that morning, while discarding the scarf and her panties in the trash, Kat wondered…What happened to me? Then, kneeling to stroke Puddy Tat's luxuriant fur, she murmured, "Thank God he never asked for our number."

Chapter 7

"Jesus, not again!"

What's wrong with me? Kat wondered, pushing aside her half-eaten breakfast for the third time that week.

"Are you all right?" Amy, her cube-mate, asked, as Kat arrived at work later that morning.

Kat tried to smile, but stopped short as a severe wave of nausea slammed into her. "God, I feel terrible," she moaned. "I must have the flu, or—"

"Well, something's wrong that's for sure," Amy interrupted, placing her hand on Kat's forehead. "I don't think you have a fever, but you look just terrible, like you haven't slept in a week."

"That's about right," Kat said, sorting through the stack of reports on her desk.

Amy watched with evident concern, until, a few moments later; Kat slowly lowered her head into her hands.

"Sweetie, maybe you should go see the nurse, this could be serious."

"Damn," Kat groaned, as she got up to leave. "What a crappy way to start the New Year."

"Can you make it by yourself?"

"I think so," Kat said, staggering down the hall. "It seems to come and go a bit."

"Okay," Amy called after her, "but let me know if I can help."

Kat felt much better by the time the nurse finished her exam. The symptoms, and the fact that she felt reasonably well most of the day, seemed to eliminate many of the usual maladies—but not all. As they sat discussing her condition, the nurse asked if there was any chance, she might be pregnant. "It sure sounds like a good case of NVP to me."

"What's that?" Kat asked cautiously.

"NVP stands for nausea and vomiting of pregnancy—in other words, morning sickness. It really sounds like that's what you've been experiencing."

"But that's not possible," Kat replied, "I mean I haven't been with anyone in a long…"

"Oh, Shit!" she exclaimed, as the ghost of her recent indiscretion flashed across her mind. "Oh that's just grand, *just fucking grand!*"

Pausing but a moment, she asked. "Isn't there some kind of test or something we can take to be sure?"

"Of course, it'll only take a moment. In the meantime, can I get you anything: coffee, tea, a Valium?"

"Cute," Kat said with a weak smile.

Kat felt kicked in the stomach when the test results came back. "What the hell am I going to do now?" She sighed.

The nurse grinned. "Have a baby I would imagine. Seriously, Kat, it's best if you start dealing with this right away."

"What do you mean?" Kat asked warily.

"Well, first off, we need to get a blood sample from the proud papa, and—"

"Sorry, no can do," she interrupted. "I don't think he's going to be very proud, or cooperative."

"That's unfortunate. There's a whole list of scary things we can protect the baby from if we know what to expect ahead of time."

Kat gave the nurse a concerned look. "Like what?"

"Well for one, he brings the possibility of hemophilia."

"Jesus! What if I can't get him to agree, is the baby in danger?"

"Not especially, Kat, but it's always best to be sure. That's why we recommend people get a blood test *before* they start fooling around."

"We were in a bit of a hurry," she said, sheepishly remembering that fateful night before Christmas.

It seems I got a present after all, she thought, Thanks a hell of a lot, Santa. See if I ever leave you cookies again.

"If push comes to shove," the nurse continued, "we can put you on some preventive medication, like folic acid, so don't worry too much. But really, you need to think hard about getting that blood sample."

"I'll try," Kat said, as she got up to leave. "I promise."

"Feeling any better?" Amy asked when Kat arrived back at her desk.

"Yes and no," Kat replied.

"What's that supposed to mean?"

"Well, it seems I've gone and gotten myself knocked up."

"Ouch! So, it was what...morning sickness?"

Kat shrugged. "Looks like it."

"Well I'm glad you're feeling better, physically at least."

"Do I know the daddy?" Amy asked. "I wonder what he'll think about all this."

"I'll bet he's not going to be pleased."

"What do you think you'll do—about the baby, I mean?"

"Have it I guess. I don't know what else to do."

"I know it's a bit early, but if you decide to discuss other options, I'd be glad to help. Unfortunately, I have some experience with that sort of thing."

"Oh Amy," Kat sighed. "Why haven't you told me this before?"

"It's not exactly the kind of thing a person talks about. Anyway, this is more about you now than me. So, are you going to see him; to let him in on the momentous news?"

"I guess I'll have to. The nurse needs a blood sample."

"Do you think he'll do it—provide the sample, I mean?"

"I don't know, but it scares the hell out of me just thinking about it." Then, "Forgive me," she apologized. "I don't mean to trouble you with my sordid little affairs."

"Trouble me? Kat, I'm your friend. We spend half our lives together in this cube. Now, why are you so scared? What's going on?"

"It may be paranoia, but something happened when we...did it. Are you *sure* you want to hear this?"

"Oh yeah, I'm all ears."

"Okay, but remember, I warned you. Anyway, we were going at it pretty hot and heavy when he began to choke me—"

"TIME OUT—I don't understand. What do you mean 'he began to choke you'?"

"Well, just as I was beginning to...climax, I felt my scarf being tightened around my throat. I remember reaching up to loosen it, but every time I did, he'd tighten it again. I was having trouble breathing and everything started getting fuzzy. Then, I guess I blacked out."

"Are you sure you weren't just imagining things?"

"I thought so, at first, but when I got home, I had these terrible bruises on my neck."

"Oh Kat," Amy sighed.

"Another thing. I woke up alone on the...where I passed out. Apparently, he just left me lying there. Doesn't that sound a bit weird to you?"

"I've heard of this before. It's some kind of kinky sex thing. In any case, it sounds like you should stay far, far away from that bastard."

"I can't. I need that damn blood sample. Oh shit, Amy, what am I going to do? I feel so incredibly stupid, stupid, stupid!"

"Don't be too hard on yourself; you're not the first woman to be taken advantage of by some creep. Anyway, Kat, please be careful."

Amy turned back to her work, then paused and asked, "You want me to keep quiet about all this?"

"Please, at least until I begin to show—if it ever comes to that."

Tio was late leaving work that evening, but Kat really didn't mind. After all, she was not exactly looking forward to seeing him. Therefore, it was with some unease that she called out to him as he strode purposefully toward his car.

"Tio, wait. Can I talk with you a minute?"

Tio's face lit up at the sight of Kat's flashing green eyes, but then, his natural wariness returned.

"It's me, Kat. Remember from the Christmas party?"

"Yeah Kat, I remember. How've you been?"

"Okay," she said, struggling to hide the apprehension in her voice.

"Listen, I've got something important to tell you."

"Yeah, like what?"

"Remember that night we were on the roof? Well, guess what, I'm pregnant."

It took Tio a moment to react to what she was saying—but only a moment.

"You're pregnant? You've got to be kidding. Didn't you use any protection—pills or something...*anything*?"

"No, I...I hadn't needed them for so long, and...and they always made me nauseous, so—"

"So you just stopped taking them, right?"

"Right," she agreed glumly.

"Not again," Tio groaned, shaking his head. "I can't believe this is happening to me *again*."

Sensing danger, Kat froze, barely breathing.

"You dumb bitch," he snapped. "You fucking

dumb bitch! So now you think you're gonna stick me with child support for the next twenty years?"

"No, it's not like that. I don't want any money. I just need a blood sample so I can protect the baby."

"Protect *what* baby? There ain't gonna be any baby. Listen to me and listen real good—get rid of it, and fast! I'm not giving any blood sample or taking any other kind of test that'll tie me to your little bastard, so get the fuck outa my face, or things will get very ugly."

Panicking, Kat reached for Tio's arm. "Please, you've got to help me!"

In the blink of an eye, Tio grabbed Kat's wrist, spun her around and slammed her up against the wall. With his other hand, he forced her head back and snarled into her ear, "I don't *have* to do anything and if you ever bother me again, Bitch, I swear I'll kill you."

Suddenly, she felt herself falling as Tio kicked her feet out from under her. As she collapsed heavily to the pavement, he placed his boot on her belly and slowly pressed down—folding her up in pain. "And if you don't get rid of this, I'll kill you both."

Leaving Kat sobbing quietly, Tio turned and walked away.

Kat was waiting in the lobby a few days later when the nurse arrived to open the clinic.

"Good morning Kat. How're you feeling?"

"Okay, I guess, but I've got bad news. I tried, but the baby's father won't give a blood sample. As a matter of fact, he doesn't want anything to do with the baby, or me, ever again."

"I'm so sorry, Kat. Maybe if you'd tell me who he

is, I might be able to help."

"No, please! Don't try to find him or pressure him in any way. He…he said he'd kill me if anyone came looking for him."

"Oh, that's ridiculous," the nurse said with a scowl. "I get stud-wannabes in here kicking and screaming all the time, but none of them has ever threatened to kill anyone. You must be mistaken."

"Please, you don't know him," Kat pleaded. "He's dangerous. He'd hurt the baby without batting an eye."

At Kat's obvious distress, the nurse relented. "All right, don't worry. We'll find a way to struggle through without him…for now."

"Thank you," Kat sighed, gathering up her things. As she did, the nurse reached out to steady her.

"Owee owee!" Kat winced as the nurse's hand closed over her bruised arm.

"What's the matter? Are you hurt?"

"No, I don't think so. It's just a less than subtle reminder from Mr. Not So Wonderful."

"Let's have a look," the nurse said, unbuttoning Kat's sleeve.

At sight of Kat's all-too-familiar black and blue pattern, the nurse frowned. I guess I underestimated him after all, she thought, watching her leave. Then, reaching for the phone, *but not anymore…*

Chapter 8

*When we look to the unborn child,
the real issue is not when life begins, but when love begins.*

—Governor Robert Casey

Tio had made his point painfully clear. A week passed since their violent meeting in the garage, and still Kat trembled. At night, she tossed and turned. During the day, she cried. At work, she spent more time looking over her shoulder than analyzing insurance trends. Finally, her hormone-enhanced paranoia convinced her to either get an abortion or jump off the roof. Deciding against the roof for the moment, Kat called for an appointment at San Antonio's Family Planning Clinic.

Later, questioning the wisdom of her fateful decision, Kat decided to talk with Amy. *She had volunteered to help after all, hadn't she?*

Amy gasped, as Kat made her unusual request. "Jesus! You've got to be kidding. I know I said I'd help, but what you're asking, would…would be very difficult for me."

"Amy, there's no one else I can trust, and I only have a couple of days to decide if I should go through with this."

"I'm sorry," Amy said, returning to her desk, "I just can't. Please don't ask me again."

In a rare moment of serenity, Amy snuggled under her favorite quilt and thumbed through a seemingly endless tome. In time, however, the intoxicating tranquility of her soft music playing in the background began to weigh heavily on her resolve. As her eyelids fluttered, Amy struggled to reread each page, then paragraph, then ultimately each line before finally lowering the book to her lap and slipping comfortably away.

Moments later, however, or were they hours? Amy could not be sure. Unwelcome voices began to insinuate their rhythm into her reverie as the familiar strains of National Public Radio's "All Things Considered" reached out to her.

"What about the political implications of the movement?" the host began. "Do you think there's anything there?"

"At this point…no," the guest responded thoughtfully. "The whole thing appears to be a non-starter."

"What do you mean?"

"Well, so far, the women's movement has proven itself to be practically impotent, without the ability either to demonstrate a collective will or to collectively exercise that will—despite controlling the vote."

"And to what do you attribute this apparent failure?"

"I think part of it can be blamed on their inability to identify a cause worth the inevitable social costs. Should the ladies ever get their act together, however, it's conceivable they could replace our entire political structure overnight."

"What does that portend for the status-quo?"

"Well for one thing, any entity, from the President on down, opposed to their agenda, should consider itself at significant political risk."

As the less than compelling discussion droned on, Amy turned once again to her book.

"...conception control instead of abortion..."

Oh, God, she thought, quickly reaching to turn up the volume. Why do they always have to go into that?

"I take it then," the host continued, "you don't really believe in woman's lib?"

"Abortion doesn't liberate women," the guest responded. "It enslaves them. It wounds their hearts, burdens their spirits and puts their souls at risk. If women truly want liberation, they should demand effective contraception—not abortions."

"It sounds like you're solidly pro-life."

"Everyone's pro-life. It's in our nature."

"I take it then that you don't believe in abortion either?"

"I view abortion in the same way I view a gun. Having one available may be an unfortunate necessity, but you had better know your heart before you use it. The damage it causes can't be taken back, and will haunt you the rest of your life."

"So it's not just about the children?"

"Oh, no, there's plenty of pain to go around: dead children, wounded mothers and a damaged society."

"So much for my nap," Amy grumbled, feeling herself drawn deeper into the conversation.

"What about Jessica McClure?"

"Now there's a name I haven't heard lately. What about her?"

"For those listeners who might not be familiar with the baby Jessica story," the host began. "She's the precious little girl who fell into a well in West Texas several years ago, and, in the process, drove sales of 'Winnie the Pooh' through the roof. Her enduring story of courage touched the hearts and riveted the attention of millions around the world."

Turning back to his guest, the host continued...

"You remember all the hoopla about her. Isn't she a perfect example of society caring deeply about its children?"

The guest pounced. "Nice try, but do you really want to know who saved little Jessica?"

"Please enlighten me," the host responded warily.

"You talk about millions. How many of those same millions would have cared a whit if that captivating child had been sucked into some high-tech vacuum cleaner instead of falling into that well? Wasn't Jessica just as precious the second before she was born as she was during that tragic ordeal, or did she somehow magically acquire a special value during her first few moments outside the womb? The reality is there wouldn't have been a child to save had she not somehow engendered a spark of love, or at least courage within her mother's breast, before that same mother chose to flush her down the drain. So if you're looking for heroes, look no further than Jessica herself. She's the warrior who won that battle, in a war that continues to be fought—and lost, every five minutes all across America."

With the mention of "courage" reverberating through her consciousness, Amy thought back to her earlier painful rejection of Kat's appeal for help.

"Fortunately or unfortunately," the host interrupted, "I don't think we're prepared to debate a woman's right to an abortion."

The guest smiled. "I thought not, especially since only those who've evaded the hideous process are left to debate it."

"Interesting point. Well folks, that's about all the time we have this morning. I want to thank you for tuning in to this special edition of 'Voices and Choices: Dissecting Women's Contemporary Issues.' As always, the opinions expressed on this program…"

As the host continued to recite the standard admonition, Amy checked the time. Then, leaning forward, she picked up the phone. Her call was short, just long enough to tell Kat once again, she would do whatever she could to help. Hanging up the phone, Amy slammed down the "off" button on her radio before pulling her knees tightly against her chest. With a long-familiar ghost sending shivers up and down her spine, she whispered angrily. "There, I said I'd help. Now, please, *leave me alone!*"

Chapter 9

To have a right to do a thing is not at all the same as to be right in doing it.
—G.K. Chesterton

"Why wouldn't you help me before?" Kat asked, reaching for her glass of tea.

Amy lowered her eyes. "I was afraid," she said, "and I still am."

"What changed your mind?"

"My damn conscience won't leave me alone."

"Conscience? What do you have to feel guilty about?"

"Never mind, let's just get this over with. What exactly do you want to know?"

"Everything, I need to know everything."

"How much do you already know?"

"Just that it hurts, emotionally I mean."

"Then why are you doing it?"

Kat groaned. "I can't see any other way out of this and it's driving me crazy. I can't sleep. My work's gone to shit. I can't even think straight. Ugh! I'm such a mess."

"Okay, but remember this was your idea." Amy flashed a quick, awkward smile. "Now where shall we begin, with conception?"

Kat playfully bumped Amy's arm. "Not that far back, silly, but everything else you can remember."

"Trust me, nobody forgets an abortion. It's been years though, so your procedure may be very different from mine."

"In what way?"

"Well for one thing, I entered the clinic through a bulletproof door. I'm pretty sure they don't have those anymore."

"Lord, I hope not. It's hard to imagine anything scarier."

"Tell me about it, especially when you're already so stressed."

"Didn't they give you anything for your nerves?"

"The attendant gave me a pill, but I still felt uneasy the whole time."

"That's understandable, considering…"

"I suppose. Anyway, after the counseling session I was okay for a while. The blood test was no big deal, and everyone was nice, but I think the sonogram was what totally tripped me out. I'd really been dreading that. I guess I just wanted to go on believing it wasn't real, but when you see it moving around inside you…"

"You watched? What was it like?"

Nervously tapping her fingers, Amy continued, "I really couldn't tell much, just a fuzzy spot that throbbed or twitched now and then. Fortunately, the sonographer noticed I was about to puke, so she let me leave."

Kat placed her hand over Amy's, the tapping stopped. "Go on," she said.

"Once I calmed down, they wrapped a paper hospital gown around my bare fanny and planted me in the waiting room—until my turn in Hell."

"Did you have to wait long?"

"No, they seemed to be running people through pretty quickly. Anyway, they finally called my number and took me into an operating room and strapped me down onto the table."

"Strapped you down?"

"Yeah, that's another thing I hope they don't do any more."

Kat grimaced. "What happened next?"

"Nothing, they just left me there with my devils."

"It must have been horrible."

"What I remember most was the cold." Amy shivered. "The worst though, was when they returned, and started poking around. I tried not to think about what was going on, what they were doing. I just couldn't focus on anything else. It's been years, but I still remember the sounds of the instruments, the antiseptic smell, and the hands…God!"

"Didn't you tell them how you felt?"

"I tried, but before I could say a word, they turned on some vacuum thingy and started suctioning me out. By that time, I'd had about enough, and just wanted to get the hell out of there, baby or no baby. I remember telling them to stop—that I'd changed my mind—but the nurse warned me not to move, and then…it was over."

Kat trembled.

Noticing, Amy whispered, "Do you want me to stop?"

"No please, I've got to know."

"Are you sure?"

"Yes, I'm sure."

Amy slowly continued, "The rest is a bit hazy, probably because I was so upset."

"They didn't just let you leave?"

"Not immediately. First they took me into some kind of recovery room and poured me into a recliner."

"Did that help?"

"Not exactly. In spite of all the soft music and subdued lighting, it turned out to be a very unpleasant place to wait. I'd thought the worst was over, but it actually felt like I'd merely replaced one burden with another."

"Oh, Amy."

"Another thing, although I'm not really..."

"Tell me, what is it?" Kat asked.

"You *sure* you're up for this?"

Kat set her chin. "I'll have to be. Now tell me."

"Well, one real young girl was holding her baby in a blanket."

"Holding her baby? You mean it wasn't dead?"

"Oh it was dead all right, but she was so far along, there really *was* something in the blanket. Not just the 'almost nothing' you'd expect."

"God!"

"The poor dear was clearly having a bad time, so they finally just took the baby away, which in itself wasn't very pleasant."

"What on earth were they thinking, closure, what?"

"Frankly, I don't believe they *were* thinking. Fortunately, it wasn't too much longer before they shoved a wad of birth control information in my hand and shooed me out the door.

"Can we stop now?" Amy pleaded, "I'm really getting depressed."

"I know it's difficult, but please tell me about afterwards."

"I'd really prefer not going there, and I'm going to hate you forever for making me."

"Amy, please!"

"Okay, but you owe me—big time. Let's see now, where was I? After I showered later that evening, it finally hit me. I noticed things were changing. My nipples were extremely sensitive, and my breasts—which before, had only begun to swell—were really engorged. When I touched them, they felt feverish. I swear it seemed like my entire body had lost its mind."

"What'd you do?"

"Nothing, I just bound my breasts like they'd told me to."

Kat leaned back in her chair. "So that was it?"

"Not entirely. Nobody warned me about how I'd feel the next day."

Kat leaned in again. "Some of that guilt you mentioned?"

"I guess so. Although it wasn't at having the abortion exactly, but that I'd killed my baby in the process. Somehow in my mind, the two things were separate."

"But it wasn't your fault."

"Oh yes it was. That's what hit me the hardest. The entire time in the clinic, all I'd thought about was what was happening to *me*. Not once did I ever think about my baby. Since then, no matter how I've twisted and squirmed—trying to blame someone or something, I've never escaped the fact that this had been *my* decision."

"But what could you have done? You were all alone."

"I don't know…something maybe…I don't know. Anyway, later that evening I removed the bindings from my breasts and stimulated my nipples, trying to make my milk come in."

"What the hell for?"

"As penance I guess, just so I wouldn't too quickly forget what I'd done."

"That's just crazy."

"Maybe. At least it's over now—for the most part."

"Amy," Kat began, "you really should have told me about this before. Maybe I could have helped."

"It wouldn't have mattered. It all happened long before you got here. Anyway, it's too late to change things now."

"I'd better go," Kat said, getting up to leave.

Suddenly Amy reached out and stopped her. "One more thing you might try. I know it may sound a bit insensitive, but why not make a list of pros and cons. That usually helps when I'm puzzled about something."

Kat gave her a hug. "Thanks Amy. I'll give it a try."

That evening, Kat curled up with a cup of hot soup and prepared her list.

- I don't think I'm mature or stable enough for a baby.
- I might not be able to care for it, unless I stop working.
- I wouldn't want it growing up in childcare.
- I couldn't stand putting it up for adoption.
- I wonder how a man feels about raising someone else's kid.
- I don't want this baby!
- *I'm scared!*

Most of the entries came easily, but some, like the last few, did not. Having exhausted all her ideas, Kat still felt the list was somehow incomplete. She wondered, in fact, whether there was something wrong with the entire list, but what could it be? She was quickly running out of time!

The fateful day had arrived. Armed with a supply of maxi pads in her apartment, Kat slowly walked up the clinic steps and reached for the heavy glass door. As she did, the realization of what was wrong with the list touched her heart. Every entry started with "I." Every entry was all about her, what *she* thought might happen, what *she* thought was important, what *she* wanted. *What about the baby?*

Jesus, Kat frowned, I'm making the same damn mistake Amy did. Kat did not completely understand her reasoning, or how long her resolve might last, but in this, the eleventh hour of her nightmare, she had finally realized, some decisions *were* best left up to God.

Chapter 10

Desperately trying to hold on to her job and the last shreds of her sanity, Kat realized she had to do everything within her power to avoid Tio. Consequently, she started going to work early and leaving late, all the while hoping he was not doing the same. With no family waiting for her at home, the extended workdays initially went well. As the demands of her pregnancy increased, however, her energy level decreased, and the long hours began to take their toll.

Early on, Kat would walk up a flight of stairs to catch the down elevator, or down a flight to catch the up elevator so she would not have to wait on her floor—exposed to the danger of running into Tio. She would also pick elevators that were at least partially full, so that she could move to the back and hide, before the elevator doors opened on her floor. This strategy had saved her more than once, as Tio entered the elevator unaware of her presence.

Time and Mother Nature inevitably caught up with her, however, as she found it increasingly difficult to manage the stairs. Forced to accept the greater risk, Kat waited for the elevator on her floor one day as Tio and a friend approached. Unable to flee, she turned from the men, and, lowering her gaze to the papers in her arms, muttered, "Damn, I knew I'd forget something." Thankfully, the men barely paused as she slowly walked away. When the elevator doors slid shut, Kat sagged against the wall and swore.

Although things went somewhat smoother after that, she still dreaded having to go anywhere near Tio's office. Unfortunately, there really was not much she could do about it, except to be extremely cautious. However, she *could* do something about another dangerous activity.

In the beginning of her pregnancy, Kat would eat in the company cafeteria as often as possible, to ensure she and the baby received some semblance of proper nutrition. Over time, however, her advancing pregnancy became more difficult to hide, and thus more frequently the subject of conversation among other patrons.

The situation finally came to a head one day, when, just as she was finishing, a voice from the past came back to haunt her.

"Why, hello, Kat. How've you been?" The Employee Relations Supervisor stopped at Kat's table. "It's been such a long time. What've you been up to?"

As she turned toward her visitor, Kat's ever-expanding tummy swiveled into view.

The supervisor smiled. "And when are we expecting this little bundle of joy?"

Anxious at the attention the supervisor's presence was attracting, Kat hesitated. "Around the end of September, if all goes well."

"Unless you know something to the contrary, my dear, I'm sure everything will be just fine. Anyway, we'll want to remember that date, won't we? How exciting," the supervisor continued. "Do you know whether it'll be a boy or a girl?"

"Not yet. So far it's a surprise."

"But do you have a preference?"

"No I really don't care," she answered, then, when a bewildered look crossed the supervisor's face, Kat quickly added, "as long as it's healthy."

"Oh yes, my dear, that's the most important thing. By the way, have you been over to fill out your maternity leave request yet?"

"No, I wasn't sure what I needed to do."

"Just come on over anytime and I'll give you a hand. I can also recommend a good OB if you don't already have one?"

Kat saddened. "I guess I haven't been preparing like I should."

"Don't worry, that's not unusual for a new mother-to-be."

"Oh, by the way," the supervisor paused as she turned to leave, "would you like for me to put a 'Blessed Event' notice in the company newsletter? It might snag a present or two."

"No, please don't," Kat said, panicking. "I'd rather wait until I'm a little further along."

The supervisor frowned. "Well, all right, but I'm sure your coworkers would love to share in your good news."

"Not all of them, I'm afraid," Kat muttered, sliding her chair away from the table.

The Southwestern Life Insurance Company was located on the edge of one of San Antonio's oldest and most beautifully wooded parks. Brackenridge, with its enclosed miniature train and amusement area, was easily a family favorite.

Each morning, its expansive, sun-drenched playgrounds teemed with happy toddlers, running through the grass or building dream castles of sand.

The joyous activity was magnetic, attracting scores of parents and parents-to-be. Within this group, Kat was eating her lunch as a young Latina hesitantly approached.

"Excuse me," Maria asked. "Do you mind if I share your bench?"

Caught in a moment of distraction, Kat answered. "No, please…"

"I love to come here and watch the children, don't you?"

"I guess. Usually I just come here to eat my lunch in peace."

"I'm sorry," Maria said with a frown. "I didn't mean to bother you."

"No, wait. That didn't sound like I intended. You're not disturbing me. I guess my mind was just a million miles away. Actually, it's kind of nice having someone to talk with."

Kat smiled, as the two women turned their attention once again to the children.

"My name's Maria by the way, Maria Vargas."

"It's nice to meet you, Maria. I'm Kat Reed."

"Kat?" Maria seemed confused. "I'm not familiar with that name. Is it like our word *gato*, the little house pet?"

"Not exactly," Kat laughed. "My 'Kat' is spelled with a 'K' instead of a 'C.' It's short for Katherine. My grandparents were the only ones who ever called me Katherine though, so 'Kat' kind of stuck."

"When are you due?" Maria asked, noticing Kat place a hand over her belly.

"What? I'm sorry, late September, if I don't get rid of the little sucker before then."

"Oh, you mustn't say such a thing," Maria gasped, crossing herself. "God is always listening."

"I was only kidding," Kat apologized. "I wouldn't do anything to hurt the baby. You're Catholic, aren't you?"

"Yes, but I don't see what that has to do with anything."

"You're right. I'm sorry for upsetting you. Please forgive me."

Maria's cheeks flushed. "No, you must forgive me for being so stupid," she said. "It's just that, well, let's forget it."

"Do you work around here?" Kat asked, relieving the tension.

"Yes, in the Southwestern Life building at the other end of the park."

"I do too. How strange we haven't run into each other before this. I come here almost every day now."

"I've only been at Southwestern a short time," Maria explained, "so I've been staying pretty close to my desk while I'm in training. Fortunately, I've reached the point where I don't feel too guilty about coming to the park for lunch, and for the children."

"Do you have any children of your own?" Kat asked.

"Oh no," she answered. "I was pregnant once, but it didn't work out."

"I'm sorry. Maybe you and your husband will have better luck next time."

"I don't have..." Maria hesitated. "I'm not married."

"That's all right," Kat said, patting her tummy and smiling. "I'm not married either."

Kat pitched the remains of her lunch to a nearby squirrel. "Well, I guess I'd better be going."

"That's too bad," Maria said with a pout. "I've been enjoying our little visit."

"So have I. Maybe I'll see you again tomorrow."

"Oh, I hope—" Maria brightened. "I mean, I'd like that."

"I'll be right here at noon," Kat said, slowly walking away.

Entering the Southwestern Life building, Kat smiled. Well, she thought, I do believe I've made my first Hispanic friend.

> April 18: Dear Diary
>
> I met someone new in the park today. She's a beautiful Anglo girl with striking green eyes. Her name's Katherine, but she prefers Kat.
>
> She seems very nice, kinda serious though, or maybe even sad. I don't think she's unhappy. It's more like she's just worried about something. She says she's not married, so maybe being alone and pregnant's the problem. Anyway, she promised to meet me again tomorrow.
>
> How strange it would be to have a gringa for a friend. Imelda'll go nuts!

Chapter 11

*Abortion is not a sign that women are free,
but a sign that they are desperate.*
—Frederica Mathewes-Green

Amy rolled her chair over to Kat's desk. "How's it going, little mommy?"

"Okay, I guess," Kat said with a smile. "At least the morning sickness has settled down a bit."

"How far along are we now?"

"Close to five months."

"Oh my, that far. Have you decided yet what to do?"

"What do you mean?"

"You know…whether to have it, or do something else."

"No, not yet," Kat said.

"Well, it's time you get serious about it. You're already into your second trimester and if you wait too much longer, things can get tricky."

"I know, but it just makes me so angry. Here I am, having to decide about some creepy abortion, merely because I couldn't take those damn pills. Jesus! What are all the doctors and researchers doing anyway? And why are things like cancer and AIDS more important than getting this birth control thing right?"

"Earth to Kat...Earth to Kat."

"Sorry..."

"That's all well and good, but you *will* have to choose, and soon—unless they don't believe in that sort of thing in Oklahoma."

"Hey, I'm as modern as the next woman," Kat complained. "It's just..."

"What?"

"It's just that none of the 'socially correct' reasons are there. It's not like I can't afford the baby, or won't take care of it, or that it's going to be horribly defective or something. It's...well, if the only reason I have for getting rid of it is that I don't want it, that just doesn't seem to be much of a reason. So, I guess my bambino and I'll have to continue on and see what happens."

"You know of course," Amy offered, "that if you decide to have the baby, you can always put it up for adoption."

"I don't know if I could stand that either—I mean my baby living with strangers. I think I'd always wonder if it was happy and being taken care of, you know, being loved. Listen to me, I almost sound maternal. Actually, I imagine any life would be better than the alternative, at least from the baby's point of view.

"Damn it, Amy. What the *hell* am I supposed to do?"

"Oh no, you don't. That's a question only you, as the baby's mother has the right to answer. I can tell you this, though: No one will suffer more than you if you get it wrong. There are all kinds of horror stories about recurring nightmares and worse—mothers actually going around for years, looking for their aborted children, that sort of thing. What I'm trying to say, is, that your conscience won't let you blame a mistake like that on someone else's bad advice. It'll know you're responsible, and it may never let you forgive yourself. So be very careful."

"But what else can I do? How on earth would I be able to raise a baby on my own?"

"People with far less than you, deal with that issue every day and do just fine. What about your folks, wouldn't they help?"

"They're both gone, and so are my grandparents. I guess it's just me and baby."

"I suppose help or advice from the papa is out of the question?"

"You got that right. He's not getting near me or my baby ever again."

"It's that bad, huh? Maybe you should just change jobs."

"I can't take the chance. If I go to another company, with a different HMO, the insurance might not go into effect for three or four months, and that's cutting it pretty close. Besides, law or no law, what employer would hire a woman who's so obviously pregnant?"

Amy sighed. "Well, let's hope something gets resolved before it's too late. One thing though, until you decide, I would recommend referring to it as the fetus, or the baby, instead of *my* baby. I know that sounds a bit harsh, but if you get too close, it'll start making you crazy."

Gently placing her hand on Kat's arm, Amy continued. "I better get back to work, but please, let me know if I can help."

Kat and Maria had been sharing lunch in the park for several weeks by the time Kat showed up, looking as if she were about to split a seam.

"God, Kat, don't you have any maternity clothes yet?"

"No, I've kind of been hoping all this pregnancy stuff was just a bad dream and that I'd finally wake up. I guess it's time to start looking into it though. I can't go on wearing these things forever."

"That's for sure," Maria said with a nod.

"Now, if I can just figure out what to get, and when."

"It looks to me like you need everything, and right now."

Kat smiled. "Well then, what do you say to a bit of shopping?"

"Great, I love to shop, especially when it's your money."

Later that afternoon, the girls visited several of San Antonio's maternity shops. In one, Maria laughed as she stretched an elastic skirt panel across her tummy.

"If you think that's funny, look at this," Kat said, holding a nursing bra up to her chest. "Actually, I don't think I'll need this. It looks just like the one my ex-boyfriend bought me for Christmas. Except, the one he gave me had holes, but no flaps."

"God, Kat," Maria shrieked, "you're terrible!"

Stepping through Kat's apartment door, Maria raised a hand to her throat. Everywhere she looked there was magic. From luxurious window treatments to the soft Persian rugs spread across gleaming Brazilian parquet floors, Maria realized she had once again entered a world far removed from any she had ever known.

"Kat, your home's beautiful."

"It's really nothing," Kat replied, sinking into an overstuffed chair and rubbing her swollen ankles.

"Nothing? Wait till you visit my place—then you'll see nothing."

"Listen, I'm starved," Kat said, changing the subject. "Let's eat before we do anything else. How about 'Italian'? I think I've got everything we'll need, including the wine."

"Uh-oh," Maria said, rolling her eyes. "I thought you weren't supposed to drink while pregnant."

"A little can't hurt," Kat said, heading for the kitchen.

"By the way," Maria called after her. "Who's this ball of fur rubbing against my ankle?"

"Oh, Maria, Puddy's never taken to anyone like that before. You must've impressed her."

After they had eaten, Maria helped Kat try on her new clothes and coordinate appropriate accessories. As Kat would change outfits, Maria passed her different combinations to try. So it was, that while selecting undergarments, Maria ran across a stunning pair of lace panties.

"Oh, my," she gasped. "What are these?"

"That, my dear, is a Tanga from Victoria's Secret. If *they* can't light a fire under your man, forget him girl, cuz he's dead." Watching Maria with the panties, Kat was puzzled to see her shiver and a tear form in her eye. "Obviously I can't wear something like that anymore," Kat said, "would you like to have them? They're brand new."

"Oh no," Maria said with a blush. "If my parents ever saw me in these, they'd skin me alive."

Kat gave her a wicked grin. "What if a man saw you in them?"

"I fear that would be far worse," Maria said, carefully laying the panties back in the drawer.

What was that all about, Kat wondered, as she pulled another new top over her head?

Later, as they talked into the evening, Kat turned suddenly, hiding a tear of her own. "Aren't we a mess," she groaned.

"Why are you crying?" Maria asked, lifting Puddy from her lap. "Is it the baby?"

"No, it's just…just that you fill my heart."

Maria reached for a tissue, wiped the tear from Kat's eye, and then, without warning, leaned forward and gently kissed her on the mouth.

"Jesus…I'm sorry," Maria stammered, as she felt Kat stiffen. "God, now you're gonna think I'm a lesbian. I keep forgetting you're not familiar with my culture.

"You dummy," Kat, laughed. "You just surprised me. I know you're not a lesbian. But, I'm pleased you care about me."

Relaxing once again, Kat leaned forward and rested her cheek against Maria's breast.

Maria gently stroked Kat's hair. "*Si*, truly you are the sister of my heart."

Kat broke the stillness of the moment. "Maria if I tell you something, something very personal, will you promise not to think badly of me?"

"Of course I won't. Now, what is it?"

"Well, just before we met, I almost did a very stupid thing. I almost had an abortion."

"You're kidding?"

"No, I'm serious. I actually got close enough to put my hand on the clinic door."

"My God, what stopped you?"

"It's kind of complicated. See I had this list."

"List? What kind of list?"

"Reasons for and against having the baby."

"Jesus, Kat, you really do need professional help."

"You noticed that too, did you? Anyway, I had this list. Wait, I may still have it here someplace."

After handing the list to Maria, Kat continued. "As you can see, it's all about me. Obviously nobody asked the baby what it thought about the abortion, or even cared what it thought, which, I now realize should have been my job."

"Why on earth would you ever consider doing something like this?"

"It's not like I've got much choice. The baby's father is threatening me."

"Who is he anyway?"

"Some bastard named Tio that I met at a Christmas party."

Maria smiled. "Tio? Are you sure his name's Tio?"

"Yes why? What's so strange about that?"

"Oh, nothing, except 'Tio' means 'uncle' in Spanish."

"'Uncle,' I thought it meant 'Theodore' or something dorky like that."

"I guess it could, but I really think he's just somebody's uncle." Leaning back against the couch, she continued. "So this was a one time thing?"

"As far as I'm concerned; although, I'm not quite sure it was for him."

"What do you mean?"

"When I confronted him with the news, he said something very odd. I think it was 'Not again,' or 'I can't believe this is happening to me again,' something like that."

"Maybe he's gotten someone pregnant before. Any idea who it might have been?"

"Not a clue, but then, there's a lot of vulnerable women in that building."

"Has he been bothering you at work?"

"Well, if you ignore the fact that I can't walk around a corner or use the elevator without having a mini-anxiety attack, or eat in the cafeteria without every bite sticking in my throat, then, not at all. But I do wish he'd stop following me home at night and screwing with my dreams."

"I get the picture. It's none of my business, but don't you have someone who can help with this? Maybe back home in…"

"Enid, Oklahoma, and nope, nobody there either."

"Oklahoma? What in God's name are you doing way down here?"

"Making a living, same as you."

"From the look of this place, you're doing that rather well. Your parents must be proud."

"They're gone. They died in an accident when I was a baby. I…I never really knew them."

"I'm sorry. Who raised you then, grandparents?"

"Yeah, but they're gone too. They passed away the year I left for college."

"I was sure you'd gone to college, you just have the look. I sometimes wish…," Maria continued wistfully, "but no, I barely made it through high school."

"Maria, you're so smart. I just know you'd make it if you went back."

"Grades aren't the problem—money is. I've got way too many bills to ever think about college."

"How can you have that many bills? You're so young."

"Shit happens…even when you're young."

I guess so, Kat thought, glancing at Maria's scars.

Finally, as the evening grew old and Maria nodded off, Kat rose and quietly went into the spare bedroom.

When she returned, Kat found Maria had awakened, and was looking at the ceramic figurine she kept on her end table.

"I see you've found my guardian angel."

"What is it really?" Maria asked. "It looks like a Christmas tree ornament, or…a finial."

"Actually, it was supposedly left for me by my mother when she died."

"Supposedly?"

"That's what my grandmother said when she gave it to me. Evidently my mother found it comforting as a child, and wanted me to feel the same."

"Does it work? Comfort you I mean?"

"Most of the time it just reminds me how alone I am."

"I'm sorry," Maria said, gently returning the angel to its table.

"Oh Kat," Maria said, looking at her watch. "It's late. I've gotta go."

"You're right, sleepyhead, it is late. In fact, it's too late. I want you to stay here tonight. I've already made up a bed and there's a gown for you in the bathroom."

"Kat are you sure? I don't mean to impose."

"You're not imposing. Besides, I'd go crazy worrying about you out on the streets alone."

"Okay, g'night," Maria said, stumbling down the hall, "and thanks."

Morning had not yet begun, as Maria, plaintively calling "Juanito! Juanito!" in her sleep, awakened Kat.

Alarmed by her cry, Kat ran to Maria's side.

"Wake up Sweetie, you're having a nightmare."

"I'm sorry Kat," Maria yawned. "I didn't mean to disturb you. I just have this crappy dream sometimes. It's really nothing."

"It didn't sound like nothing to me. Who's Juanito?"

"Juanito…Juan, was the love of my life, but he's dead now."

"I'm sorry, was he the father of your baby?"

"No, it's a long story. I promise I'll tell you someday, but…"

Undeterred, Kat continued. "It sounded like there was a child in your dream. Was it yours?"

"I think so. I don't know." Maria began to cry. "Kat, I'm so scared."

Kat took Maria's hand. "Maybe you'd better come to bed with me for a while."

After settling in, Maria reluctantly revealed more of her past.

"About a year ago, I was raped. I almost died…and I can't have any more children."

"Any more? Then you did have a child."

"No not really. I got pregnant from the rape, but it didn't work out."

"What do you mean?"

"Don't hate me, Kat, but I did the same thing you thought about doing—I had an abortion. It seemed necessary at the time, but now I'm not so sure. It might just have been another tragic mistake. Anyway, I survived it…sort of."

"Sort of?"

"Well, a lot of things are different now."

"Like what?" Kat gently probed.

"Emotional things, you know; feelings, personal relationships…"

"You mean *men*."

"Yeah. Actually it's probably for the best, since my doctor told me I could die if I get pregnant."

"Things are pretty torn up inside, aren't they?" Kat whispered.

"I guess so, in more ways than one."

"Well, we'll just have to share this baby," Kat offered. "What do you think about that?"

"I think that might be difficult," Maria said with a smile.

"Piece of cake. By the way, it's your turn for morning sickness."

Maria pouted. "Hey, no deal!"

"Feeling better now?" Kat asked.

"Kat, you're a wonder. Now, is there anything you can do about my faith in God?"

"What do you mean?"

"Ever since the rape, well, really since my abortion, I've had this almost mystical feeling that God has a special plan for me, something...Anyway, nothing's happened. I've begun to wonder if I'm not just being stupid again."

"Maria, you mustn't say that. Someone has to keep the faith for us. Besides," she asked, "doesn't the Bible say something about 'In God's own good time'?"

Maria smiled. "You're close."

Chapter 12

With her pregnancy progressing, it became clear that Kat was finding it more and more difficult to care for herself. When her condition began to be noticed at work, Amy became concerned.

"Kat, you've just got to do something, people are beginning to talk."

"I know Amy, but when I get home at night, all I can do is fall into bed."

"You know I'd be glad to help."

"You're a dear, but I really have to find the strength to deal with this myself—other people do."

"That may be true, Kat, but most of them have someone at home to help."

"I have help. I have Puddy Tat."

"Very funny. At least let me do your hair in the morning so you won't look like you've been sleeping under your desk. And for God's sake, bring me your laundry!"

With Amy's help, Kat's work situation began to improve. At home, however, things turned deadly.

"Oh great, here we go again," Kat groaned, rushing into the bathroom for the second time since breakfast.

"I sure hope this isn't more of your morning sickness, Bambino, because if it is, you're really pressing your luck."

Realizing she was too ill for work, Kat picked up the phone.

"Amy, I feel like shit and I've been puking all morning. I think I'd better stay home—at least for today."

"Have you seen a doctor?"

"Not yet, but if things get much worse, I'll try and find one."

"*Find one?* Dare I ask who's been doing your prenatal care?"

"Don't be mad at me Amy," Kat whimpered. "I'm very pregnant, and I don't feel good, and—"

"Well first things first," Amy interrupted. "When you decide it's time, just call HR. and—"

"HR? What's Human Resources have to do with this?"

"They'll set up an urgent care authorization, so you can come in and see the company quack."

"Thanks, Amy. What would I ever do without you?"

"Just call, so I don't have to worry."

"Okay," Kat promised, reaching for the company directory.

After finding the number, Kat placed the call. When the employee relations representative picked up the phone, however, his voice seemed ominously familiar. In her current state, it took Kat's mind a few moments to remember—"Jesus, Tio works in HR!"

Fortunately, she had not given her name. So, after mumbling, "Forget it…I'll be fine…thanks anyway," she slammed down the phone.

Damn, everywhere I turn that bastard's right in my face, she thought. He even has his tentacles in the company's medical system. There's no way I can take the chance of seeing a doctor now.

Maria was concerned. She had not heard from Kat in two days, which was unusual. Unable to contain herself any longer, she grabbed the phone.

"Hi Amy, it's Maria, is Kat there?"

"No Maria, she called in sick yesterday morning, and I haven't heard from her since."

"Kat's sick? What's wrong with her?"

"I don't know, but she sounded pretty bad when she called. I told her to go and see the company doctor, but I don't know how that turned out. Do you think you could go over and see about her? I was going after work, but if you could go sooner, I'd sure feel better."

"Don't worry, I'll check on her. Something must be up, or she would have called one of us by now."

Maria rang Kat's doorbell for what seemed like an eternity, before she finally heard the lock click.

"Jesus, Kat, what's wrong with you? You look like the devil."

Kat sagged against the doorframe. "Maria! Thank God, you're here. I don't feel well, and…and I think there's something wrong with the baby."

"What do you mean?"

"I've been having terrible cramps, and there's some blood."

"Oh, God," Maria said, as Kat pitched forward and retched.

Placing her palm against Kat's forehead, Maria frowned. "You're burning up. How long have you been like this?"

"I can't...I don't remember. Maria, please help me!"

"Sweetie, shouldn't you maybe see a doctor?"

"I can't. If I make a request through the HMO, Tio might hear about it. If he recognizes my name, he could find my address in the files—I am *so* screwed."

Maria appeared deep in thought for a moment, before brightening. "Maybe there's another way. I'll call my aunt in Bandera, she's a nurse."

As Maria explained Kat's symptoms, Virginia told her it sounded like Salmonella.

"I'll be there as soon as I can," Virginia said, clearly concerned. "In the mean time, don't touch anything in the kitchen, or anywhere else for that matter."

While waiting for Virginia, Maria bathed Kat and changed her gown.

After examining Kat, Virginia grabbed Maria and headed for the kitchen.

"I've got a bad feeling about this, whatever it is. She's obviously too sick to care for herself. If she doesn't have some help, at least temporarily, I'm afraid she may very well miscarry."

"I'll look after her, Auntie; just tell me what needs to be done."

Virginia smiled as she began dumping Kat's fluorescent leftovers in the trash. "I thought that's what you'd say."

Her aunt's instructions were simple; clean and sterilize everything, including Kat.

"No telling what she's got growing around here, so you might as well toss the rest of her food. As for Kat, you have to watch her fever carefully—it's essential for the baby. If it spikes, put her in the tub. She's not going to like it, so you'll have to be tough. She'll probably have headaches, diarrhea, and more vomiting, the whole bit. How long did you say she's been ill?"

"About three days I think. Any idea when we should see some improvement?"

"With proper care, she might turn around pretty quickly, maybe in a couple of days."

As good as her word, Maria cared for Kat from early morning until late at night. Kat never had so much chicken soup in her life. In between, Maria scrubbed the kitchen, the bath, and every other surface Kat might have touched.

On Sunday morning, Kat finally awakened without the blinding headache she had suffered with most of the week. Turning slowly, drawn by the sunlight filtering through her window, she noticed Maria, still fully dressed, asleep in the chair by her side. Running her fingers through Maria's hair, Kat thought about how dangerous the situation had become. It was obvious, that by trying to manage everything herself, she had inadvertently placed her baby at risk.

Although she had never been there, Kat knew Maria lived in a modest rented room somewhere across town. She also knew how lonely Maria had been since arriving in San Antonio—just as she had.

"If only...," Kat whispered.

"If only what?" Maria murmured, raising her head and smiling. "Well, you're looking better, how do you feel?"

"Oh *much* better, except, do you think you could maybe move in here just in case I have a relapse?"

"What are you talking about? What kind of relapse?"

"The simple truth is, Maria, that without you, I'm afraid I'll just get my sorry ass in trouble again."

"You really want me to move in here?"

"Yes! The other bedroom is going to waste, and we'll have so much fun. Besides, I do need you."

"Are you sure you're not just fishing for a free 'Mescan' maid and full-time baby sitter?"

Smiling, Kat countered. "Actually, it's more like giving you a chance to do your Catholic duty, looking after a poor white-trash gringa and her half-breed bastard."

"Umm, I'm gonna tell Baby," Maria said with a snicker, then, seeming to reflect but a moment, relented.

"Okay, I'll move in with you, on one condition."

"What? I'll promise anything," Kat begged. "Just stay with me—please, oh, please."

"Promise me you'll be good!"

"Oh, poo," Kat said pouting. "I should've seen that coming."

Chapter 13

"Damn!" the priest mumbled, as the night-confession bell rang in the church office at the far end of the hall.

Slowly rising from his pillow, he turned toward the clock and groaned, "Who could possibly want absolution at this ridiculous hour?"

The priest paused for a moment to work on the knot that had recently taken up painful residence at the back of his neck. Then, slipping out of his nightshirt, he stumbled across the room for his soutane. Just then, the unwelcome bell pealed its insistent demand yet again.

"Keep your shirt on," he grumbled, quickly buttoning the robe. "I'm coming as fast as I can."

Stepping into the semi-darkened sanctuary, he immediately noticed the red light glowing on one of the confessionals. The solitary "occupied" light shining in a sea of gloom would have been noteworthy in any case, but, in this instance, it meant someone had gained access to a switch, normally locked away within the priest's private compartment.

Upon entering the confessional, the priest wearily crossed himself and began, "In the name of the Father and of the Son and of the Holy Spirit. Amen."

Settling back on the well-worn bench, he suddenly felt a wave of dread wash over him, as…

"Father…"

The abruptness startled him. "Yes…yes, my son?"

"You seem weary, Father," the voice began. "Why is that?"

"Well, it is an unusual hour for a confession."

"Is that the only reason?" the voice asked, ignoring his implication.

The priest hesitated, staring intently at the shadowy countenance in the penitent's compartment. But, finding himself strangely unable to resist, offered, "Actually, I…I haven't been sleeping well lately, but that's another story. Now, shall we begin?"

"If you wish…"

If I wish? He thought. This was your idea, not mine.

The specter continued, "Father…"

"Yes, my son? What *is* it?"

"You seem troubled as well. Why is that?"

The priest once again surrendered to the haunting presence. "It's just something that happened, something that's been bothering me."

"Something…with Maria?"

Stunned, the priest gasped. "How…how did you—"

"Shall we continue?"

"I'm not so sure we should," the priest cautioned.

"It's all right, Father," the voice soothed. "Please continue."

Unconvinced, the priest asked, "Why are you here,

if not for absolution?"

"On the contrary, Father, absolution is exactly why we're here. Now, what has happened to burden you so?"

The priest reached for the compartment door, but then paused once again. "Confessions are sacred. Surely you know that."

Disregarding the priest's admonition, the unrepentant voice continued. "Maria confessed her sins, you absolved her. Why are you so burdened?"

"No," the priest sighed, "that's the problem, she wasn't forgiven. I never had a chance to—"

"Never had a chance?"

"She left before I could finish."

"Did you not go after her?"

"No, what good would've come of that?"

"You might be sleeping better," the voice whispered.

"It isn't possible now anyway. I've heard she's left Bandera."

"She will return. Watch for her."

"How can you know that?"

"It doesn't matter," the voice continued. "What does matter is why she fled Bandera in the first place."

"I'm afraid I may have driven her away, although that clearly wasn't my intent. I thought she understood what I was trying to—"

"It seems to me, you were trying to send her straight to Hell."

"No, I—"

"You did deny her absolution, didn't you?"

"I told you, she left before…" The priest paused.

"We shouldn't be discussing this."

"You're still angry with her, aren't you?"

"Don't you realize we could be excommunicated?"

"Ah, yes, the ever present threat; kind of a waste you know."

"A waste?"

"You priests expend so much energy warning sinners of the torments of Hell, when it seems to me, that not going to heaven is punishment enough."

"Please, why are you here?"

"To help you."

"Help me? Help me with what?" the priest asked.

"Your confession."

"*My confession*? You're the one being confessed here. I haven't done anything to—"

"Nothing except condemn a soul to eternal damnation."

"What? What do you mean? Who *are* you?"

"The messenger is not important."

"Messenger?" the priest scoffed. "What message could you possibly have for me?"

"A simple one. '*Judge not, that ye be not judged.*'"

Trembling, the priest cautiously rose and exited the confessional.

As he reached into the penitent's compartment, placing his hand on the kneeler, he found it cool to the touch.

"I thought so," he groaned.

The priest entered his bedroom and stood for a moment,

before glancing down and realizing he was still in his nightshirt. Remembering the clock, he again checked the time, his worst fear confirmed. Only a single moment had passed since the bell had awakened him from his sleep.

"It was a dream," he muttered. "Only a dream, yet it seemed so real."

Chapter 14

> ... *a procedure many decent and civilized people find so abhorrent as to be among the most serious of crimes against human life.*
> —Justice Anthony M. Kennedy - Stenberg v. Carhart

Nearing the end of yet another steamy South Texas afternoon, Kat walked through the open doorway and turned toward the elevators at the end of the hall. As she traversed the lengthening beams of light, her heart leapt into her throat. For within their dancing shadows, Kat saw the telltale reflection of someone approaching from Tio's corridor.

She turned and frantically ran toward her only avenue of escape. Bursting through the men's room door, she slipped out of her heels and stepped silently into the nearest stall.

Kat climbed onto the toilet and balanced herself between the partitions, just as Tio and a man, whose voice she did not recognize, entered the room—crossing to the urinals along the wall.

"So, what's the problem this time, Tio?" the stranger asked.

"Oh the usual, some bitch over in Accounting got her feelings hurt and wants to hang me out to dry."

"What is it with you? Can't you just fuck 'em without all that kinky crap?"

Tio chuckled. "I guess not."

"Aren't you worried the supervisor will get wind of your little 'sexual problem'?"

"She ain't gonna find out. I've worked too hard to get where I am, to let some woman fuck me up."

"What're you going to do about this one?"

"Nothing, she's just blowin' smoke. She knows if she ever said anything, I'd make her regret it for the rest of her short, painful life."

"You suck," the stranger snarled.

Tio headed for the door, but then stopped. "What's that smell?"

Kat cringed and imagined him turning toward her.

"Jesus, Tio, it's a john. What kind of question is that?"

"No, this is different. It's like perfume, and it seems…somehow familiar."

"Now you've been doing the cleaning lady? You really are pathetic."

Kat leaned her head against the wall and exhaled sharply as the two men laughed and left the room.

Hurrying into the complex, Maria noticed Kat's car parked askew in front of their apartment—justifying her earlier concern.

Normally, the two women rode to work together, so it was unsettling when Kat failed to pick her up that afternoon.

Upon entering the apartment, she searched from room to room until finding Kat, slumped in the corner by her bed, the phone buzzing in her lap.

"Sweetie," Maria asked, returning the phone to its cradle. "What's happened?"

"Oh Maria, it's just horrible." Kat shivered. "I can't let them do that. I just can't!"

"What's wrong? What are you talking about?"

As Kat lowered her eyes, Maria noticed the card gripped tightly in her hand. Taking the card, Maria's heart sank as she recognized the clinic's imprint on its surface.

"Oh, Girlfriend," she sighed, "what've you done?"

"I needed to know what would happen, if…if I couldn't protect my baby from Tio."

"So you called those murderous bastards at the—"

"The baby doesn't have a chance," Kat snapped. "Let's face it, Maria. If Tio finds us, he'll drag me into that horrid place, and they'll kill my baby, and there won't be a damn thing I can do about it."

"So that's what you believe? That there's no hope?"

"Just show me it's not going to happen. Convince me, Maria, the baby has even one chance in Hell of surviving all this—just one!"

Maria looked past Kat's pain, and softened. "Tell me, did something happen at work?"

"I heard him. He said he was going to hurt me," Kat whimpered.

"You talked to him…to Tio?" Maria gasped.

Kat took a deep breath. "No, not directly, but I got trapped in the men's room and—"

"What were you doing in the men's room?"

"Hiding from Tio. I almost bumped into him in the hall and there wasn't any other place to go. I overheard him tell some guy, he was after a woman who'd threatened him."

"Are you sure he was talking about you?"

"No, it wasn't about me," Kat said. "This girl's in Accounting, but it easily could've been."

"Jesus, Kat, take a pill, you really had me scared. Now, what's this other thing you were talking about?"

Kat regained her composure. "Remember when we were doing that research about abortions, and we found all those survivor stories on the Internet? Well they're nothing compared to what I was just told over the phone. They said, since I was so far along, I'd have to have something called a partial-birth procedure."

"What's that?"

"It's for women who can't, or won't get an abortion until late in their pregnancy. Anyway, it's horrible."

"You already said that," Maria scolded. "Now, what exactly is it?"

"The woman on the phone said during the abortion, they'd use forceps to pull the baby—except for its head—out of my body. Then they'd stab a hole at the base of its skull and suck its brains out until the head collapses."

"Jesus, Mary, and Joseph! Why would they do that?"

"She said it's the only way to take a late-term baby without going to jail for murder."

"I swear, Maria, when I heard that, it felt as if my heart had stopped."

"I can't believe there's such a thing," Maria said, crossing herself.

"We have to believe it. Why would she lie?"

Maria shuddered. "Who would be so desperate, as to consider such a thing?"

"The woman on the phone said thousands have done it. How could there be so many, and yet we've never heard about it?"

"Maybe it's only done in life-and-death situations," Maria offered.

"If you call being 'depressed' a life-and-death situation, then I guess that's true."

"You're kidding. They'd really accept depression as justification for doing something like that?"

"I had to practically force it out of her, but...yes, that's what she said."

"Maybe that's why we haven't seen it on the news."

"Well, it's good enough for me," Kat hissed. "I'm getting a fucking gun. They're going to have to kill me before those bastards get their hands on *my* baby."

"Don't talk like that, Kat, you're giving me the creeps."

"You're right. We need to get off this—it's not healthy."

"Didn't anything *good* happen to you today?" Maria pleaded.

"Maybe one thing. Guess who's kicking again."

"You're kidding. What's it like this time?"

"It's very different from the fluttering I felt before; this is *much* stronger."

"Ohhh, Kat, remember you promised to share."

Chapter 15

*The most merciful thing that a family does to
one of its infant members is to kill it.'*

—Margaret Higgins Sanger – Founder, American Birth Control
League [Planned Parenthood]

She came to him before dawn on that fateful day, while the rest of her family lay sleeping. He had stayed over the evening before, dozing on the couch in the room next to hers, so near and yet…

He was with her now, but in the morning, he would be gone, off to school in the East. His, was the second step in their plan for the rest of their lives, the first of which had been to fall in love. The third step would be for her to join him in the spring. They hoped, in time, to room "near," yet not "with" one another. To do otherwise was too dangerous a step, a step best left for others to tread. Those were issues for the future, however, for another time. For now, her focus was on fear.

Earlier, as she lay in her bed listening to the rhythmic sounds of his breathing, she had slowly realized the risk she was taking by letting him go off alone. A lot could happen in a year to strain the delicate bond between them.

Would he remember her after he had gone? And, if so, what vision would he see? Would the memory of an adolescent kiss, or her budding breasts pressing against him in the dark, be enough to hold his heart?

Easing quietly out of bed, she crossed to the chest against the wall, the wall keeping them apart, knelt and removed the gown. Slipping out of her tee shirt and shorts, she quickly wiped her body clean of the remnants of sleep—and of her fear. It would not do for him to sense the measure of her dread. Then, reaching into the drawer one last time, she retrieved her panties. After all, there's only so much a girl can invest in creating a dream.

She leaned over his outstretched body, and gently placed her hand on his heart. In doing so, her gown—rich with its heady perfume—fell away from her virginal body and slowly descended over him, robbing him of the ability to speak, even to breathe. At her touch he stirred, and, reaching into the darkness, pulled her down…down onto his awakening body, down onto his awakening need.

As she sat in the stairwell, huddled against the early morning chill, she could not remember when she had removed the panties, although she was sure it had been her idea. For even under the power of his passion, she was certain he would never have taken advantage of her, no matter how desperately she had wanted him to—for that was not part of their plan. But that was then, and this was now.

Waiting in the dawn, she marveled at how such a beautiful dream could have gone so terribly wrong, and yet there it was, shattered in pieces at her feet. Gone…because of the baby.

She had not told him, of course, because of his damned nobility. She knew he would immediately leave school to be with her, to support her, then possibly someday learn to regret, and to blame her. Anyway, it was just easier this way...without him. This way, she could do whatever was necessary to save his life, even if it meant destroying hers—and their baby.

The easy part was obtaining the phone number and making the call; keeping her nerve up had been harder. In fact, everything had gone according to plan until "they" arrived to block her path.

First the horrible signs appeared, carried by a few early-risers. If the clinic had been open by then, she felt certain she could have entered without being seen. In time, however, their numbers grew to the point where entry without being accosted was no longer possible.

And so, she remained in the stairwell, contemplating her fate, limited it seemed to the bitter end of a rusty coat hanger.

Merging onto the North Loop, Maria groaned.

"Must be an accident," she said, noticing the ribbon of lights streaming off into the distance. "Maybe we'd better try a different way."

Creeping along in the right-hand lane, she finally exited, turning south onto San Pedro and back into the city.

"This looks better," Maria said with a smile.

Kat, on the other hand, was not so pleased. "Shit," she grumbled, suddenly realizing where they were, and where they would be going.

"What's the matter?" Maria asked.

"The clinic's this way."

"Where you went for the abortion?"

"That's the one."

"Want me to turn around?" Maria offered.

"No, I'll be all right. We're going to be late as it is."

"How far is it?"

"We're there," Kat said. "It's the building on the ...Oh, look at all those people."

"Who do you suppose they are?" Maria asked, alarmed by the crowd at the entrance.

"Considering all the signs, protestors I would imagine...and they have cameras."

"Why on earth? ...," Maria asked.

"I've heard they take pictures of women trying to enter the building and post them on the Web to scare others away. Apparently it works too, because I don't see any customers, except...Maria, stop the car!"

As Kat slipped out and ran toward the parking garage, Maria called after her. "Maybe we shouldn't get involved."

In what seemed only seconds, Kat returned—her face flush with excitement—and reached for the umbrella.

Maria grabbed her arm. "What're you *doing*?"

"Don't worry; I'll be right back. Just keep the motor running."

Returning to the stairwell, Kat used her umbrella to shield the young girl, as she entered the clinic.

Moments later, Kat jumped into the car as Maria, frantic to evade the blossoming flashbulbs, sped away.

"Jesus, Kat, you shouldn't have done that."

"I had to. She was going to abort the baby herself if she couldn't get into the clinic."

"Why would she try such a dangerous thing?"

"She wouldn't tell me everything, but...Oh, Maria, I just couldn't leave her there."

"Kat, don't you realize what a terrible chance you're taking with God?"

Kat smiled. "I can't get over how real He is for you. You're right, I'm sorry. I'll try to be more careful in the future—at least until after the baby's born."

"Dammit, Kat, you know it doesn't work that way! Sometimes I feel I can't trust you anymore. You're always apologizing, and then going and doing the wrong thing anyway. I'm warning you. If you don't start taking this seriously—"

"I said I was sorry," Kat interrupted.

An awkward moment passed before she continued, "Maria, do I look really fat?"

"Why do you care? You're six months pregnant for Christ's sakes."

"Well, I was just wondering how I'll look on the Internet."

Maria groaned.

June 20: Dear Diary

I'm getting scared. This morning Kat helped a young girl get an abortion. I have the feeling she still regrets not having done it herself, months ago. She's worried about what will happen if she isn't able to protect the baby from Tio. I've tried to tell her everything will be all right, but she doesn't believe me.

I need a new plan...

Chapter 16

And then to see, to be with somebody while they're having the injection when they're twenty or twenty-four weeks, and you see the baby moving around, kicking around, as this needle goes into the stomach, you know.'
—Susan Lindstrom, W.S.W., Clinic Worker

Maria dozed intermittently as a lonely cricket chirped its solitary song somewhere off in the distance. Her sleep, burdened by anticipation, had not come easy. Finally, the phone chimed a merciful death to her nocturnal pursuit. Turning her bedside light up a notch, she listened intently, until…

"Yes, I understand. We'll be there as soon as we can."

Maria tiptoed across the cool parquet floor and lowered herself onto the side of Kat's bed. As if sensing her presence, Kat eased herself up onto an elbow. "What's wrong? Are you all right?"

"Hurry and get dressed. I've got a surprise."

Kat checked the time. "You're kidding, isn't it a bit early for surprises?"

"Oh, come on, you'll love it."

Although apprehensive, Kat sat quietly as they drove across town. When Maria turned into the hospital district, however, her growing unease prevailed. "Maria, what's going on?"

"Don't worry; we're just here for a sonogram."

"A sonogram? But why?"

"Aunt Virginia thought it best we make sure the baby's all right...since you were so sick and all."

"Aren't you forgetting Tio?"

"This one's off the record. Auntie's got connections."

"But what if someone sees us?"

"That's why we're here so early. Auntie's friend, Shannon, works the nightshift. There shouldn't be anyone around to worry about."

"I hope you're right," Kat mused, concern still lingering in her voice.

Thanks to her conversation with Amy, Kat was vaguely familiar with the procedure she was about to undergo. Still anxious, she settled onto the gurney and turned her head toward the blank display. Fortunately, it took Shannon only a few seconds to slide Kat's jeans down and slather her swollen belly, before the screen lit up in a succession of ghostly images swooping in and out of view.

Kat gasped, as the screen suddenly snapped into focus. "Is that the baby?"

Shannon smiled. "Yup, that's it."

"It looks so weird," Maria said, "almost as if you can see right through it."

"You can...sort of," Shannon said, carefully scanning the baby from head to toe. "If it'll settle down, that is."

"It *has* been kicking the crap out of me lately."

"Yeah, things get a bit cramped at this stage," Shannon said. "Speaking of that, let's measure its femur to see how far along you are."

While Shannon placed the crosshairs at the appropriate points, Kat seized the opportunity to ask the question that had been foremost on her mind.

"Can you tell if…if the baby's all right?"

"I don't think you have to worry," Shannon replied. "The level of movement and heart rate are as expected, and the physical measurements are all within their norms. She or he appears to be doing just fine."

Kat squinted at the display. "Can you tell what it is?" she asked.

"Kat," Maria interrupted, "are you sure you wanna know?"

"I think so. We may not have another chance before we paint the nursery."

Maria scowled. "I figured that's why you'd ask."

The display swooped out of focus once again. "If baby'll cooperate," Shannon said, "we'll try and find out."

"Uh-oh," she giggled. "Looks like someone's peeing."

The women craned their necks to peer into the swirling fluidic display as footsteps shuffled in the hall.

Maria frowned. "Maybe we'd better go."

"She's probably right," Shannon agreed, pressing the machine's print button. "It's best to be careful, considering your situation."

As Kat slid off the gurney, Shannon slipped the printout into her pocket.

"What's this?" Kat asked, glancing down.

Shannon smiled. "Something for later."

Arriving at the car, Kat immediately flipped on the dome light and reached into her coat.

"What'd she give you?" Maria asked.

"Our first baby picture. Jeez, you can see almost everything; fingers, toes, everything except…"

"Except what?"

Kat smiled. "His thingy."

"So, we still don't know?"

"Nope," Kat groaned. "I guess we'll just have to wait."

Maria slipped the car into gear, "Good, I'd rather be surprised."

"As if making it to delivery won't be surprising enough."

"Will you stop," Maria grumbled. "Sometimes you…Oh, never mind."

"Are you ever going to tell me the real reason we just went through that exercise?" Kat asked, as they drove into the dawn.

"What do you mean? I told you, Virginia was—"

"Maria…" Kat's tone rose an octave, as if catching a child in a lie.

"I was afraid," Maria relented. "I wanted you to see—"

"See what?"

"You know, that the baby was…real"

"But why?"

"So you wouldn't do something…something without thinking."

Considering her comment for a moment, Kat began. "That was a precious thing you did for me, and I know you meant well, but…"

Breathless, Maria asked, "But what?"

"I wish you'd find it in your heart to trust me a little more."

Chapter 17

You cannot discover the purpose of life by asking someone else - the only way you'll ever get the right answer is by asking yourself.
—Terri Guillemets

Maria's right, it's time…probably way past time.
Her words had settled deep within Kat's mind ever since their confrontation earlier that morning. Kat felt she knew why. It was one thing to haggle over what to do about dinner, but hesitating so long on such an important decision? Well, that was another thing entirely.

Was it Maria? she wondered. Maybe the desire to please her was getting in the way, confusing the issue. *She's always there, trying to help…needing to help.* Did she not realize her involvement would never relieve Kat of the ultimate responsibility, or ease her pain if things went wrong?

She tried to explain when dropping Maria off at the apartment after work. "Some things need to be done alone," she had said. "Some things need sorting out."

Kat should have saved her breath. Maria was bound to worry, and yet, there was little, if anything she could do since Kat asked her "to trust a little more."

The streets were crowded as Kat headed back toward town. Fortunately, most of the traffic was going the opposite direction, people rushing home to their families, to their children.

Struggling to focus, Kat slipped into a parking spot at the River Walk off Soledad. Whispering a short prayer for luck, she exited the car and quickly made her way to the old stone steps leading down to the river. The River Walk was a godsend. Few other places would allow her to mingle unnoticed, yet afford so many avenues of escape.

It seemed like years since Kat last visited the river. Still, she was amazed at her feelings as she left the hubbub of the streets, and descended into the tranquility below. Above, the air was heavy with the smell of exhaust, yet here, there was only the aroma of flowers and the muted sound of waiters serving their guests.

Kat smiled, knowing the contrast was merely an illusion, at best. Soon, hordes of prowling singles and excited tourists would invade her Eden yet again. Nevertheless, for now she could stroll in relative peace, struggling with her demon. Actually, there were two questions, she realized, one, *life or death*, the other, *life ever after*.

Maybe dealing with each issue separately would help, she decided. After all, "One cross at a time," her grandmother used to say. Speaking of help, Kat wondered if God would be with her on this, or leave her in the hands of devils. One thing was certain; she was *not* alone now, as her bladder kept reminding her. "Please stop jumping," she begged her child within, while searching restaurants for an open door.

Moments later, Kat entered a café and headed for the ladies room. The quick glance she took as she hurried along was not very comforting. "I hope it's not a dump," she grumbled, pushing open the door with her foot. Her fear was unfounded, as the room seemed surprisingly clean. Good, she thought, breathing a sigh of relief, I'm getting way too heavy to hover.

Exiting the stall, Kat paused to stare at her reflection in the mirror. "Thank God for Maria," she murmured, studying the worry lines at her mouth and dark circles under her eyes. "I can imagine what a mess I'd be without her."

A baby's compelling cry reached out to her as she reentered the café. Instinctively turning toward the infant's distress, she stopped in her tracks. Within the shadows along the wall, she glimpsed a young girl trying to calm one baby while feeding another at her breast. As Kat's eyes adjusted to the gloom, she realized the girl was returning her stare, matching it with an intensity she found unsettling. Captured by the stranger's eyes, Kat swallowed hard before taking a tentative step into the dark.

With Kat obviously pregnant and suitably intimidated, the girl softened her look. "Name's Ram," she said with a slight smile, "short for Ramona."

"Ram," Kat, replied, "interesting nickname, mine's Kat."

"Kat, huh?" Ram's smile widened. "I imagine assholes have just as much fun with yours as they do with mine."

Distracted once again by the commotion, Kat offered to help. Leaning to entice the unhappy infant with a bottle, Kat studied its mother out of the corner of her eye. She appeared to be in her late teens or early twenties at most. Short, unstyled hair framed a pleasant, though not particularly pretty face, dominated by dark brown eyes and a tear-shaped 'tat' on her cheek. Tight, ragged jeans, sandals, and a well-worn maternity top completed the picture of a hard rock candy kind of life.

Later, thinking back, Kat would not remember how it all began, but one thing naturally led to another, until the girl offered her story: Mexico was home. She'd come across the Rio Grande late one night with her older sister. Wasn't long before she took up with a gang and got passed around. Actually they'd used each other, the men for prestige, she for protection. Boyfriends evaporated (thank God) when she started throwing up each morning. Not that she cared, never sure who the father was anyway. First thing she thought about when she realized she was pregnant, was where to get a gun. Then one day she met an old white lady needing her house cleaned and someone to talk with. She'd worked right up to delivery. Twins were a surprise, since there hadn't been any prenatal care to speak of. Week later she'd returned to the streets, but this time with two babies strapped to her back.

"You're an illegal?" Kat asked, looking around to see if anyone had overheard. "Aren't you afraid of getting caught?"

"Nah! INS won't touch me with a ten-foot pole now I've got the twins. They couldn't stand the heat."

Kat gazed at the baby in its mother's arms. "There's so much to learn."

"You'll be fine. Just remember, there's only about five things they'll do: eat, sleep, cry, poop…and love. I've never felt such love."

"Tell me about your sister," Kat asked softly.

Ram paused before continuing. "There isn't much to tell, except she always looked out for me."

"Ever wonder what happened to her?"

"I *know* what happened to her," Ram responded, turning her head to hide a tear.

Kat changed the subject. "How do you survive?"

"It's not so bad. I have work and my room, and these guys keep me pretty busy. I just hope God'll help, even if it's only with beans and baby food."

"That's not what I meant…what about the babies? Ever wonder what's best for them?"

A pained look came over Ram's face, as if Kat had slapped her. "You fuck!" she growled, holding the child closer. "Maybe you think giving them up would be better?"

"I'm sorry," Kat said. "I didn't mean…"

Visibly shaken, Ram seemed not to hear. Staring uncomfortably at Kat, she continued. "Sometimes, I do get scared for them. Sometimes I have to fake shit, like I'm really brave, and hope somehow I can be."

"But why?" Kat asked softly.

"You still don't get it, do you? I'm their mother." The edge in her voice quickly returned. "You need to leave now."

"I'm so sorry," Kat repeated, sensing how deeply her words had hurt.

"I know, Chica," Ram said, "but you need to go …and think about that abortion."

Surprised, Kat gasped. "I never said…what makes you think…?"

"It's written all over your lily-white face."

Walking slowly back to her car, Kat thought about what had just happened. *How could she know—really know—what was in my mind?* And the baby, something very special happened there as well. Some kind of electricity had passed between them when she reached out to touch him. She could still feel his warmth, the smell of him, and those innocent dark eyes—looking up at her—looking through her—as she fed him. Finally, there had been the tiny fingers wrapping around her thumb. "Oh God," Kat sighed, remembering his touch.

Suddenly the vision of a hand reaching for the clinic door flashed across her mind.

"I can't do that again," she cried. "I won't!"

Straightening, Kat stared down the path before her as if seeing it for the very first time. Her heart raced and she felt faint. It seems we *are* going to have a baby after all, she decided, but then, what about the rest…the 'life ever after' part?

"I'll think about that tomorrow."

Kat entered the car and then paused, her hand on the ignition key. Releasing her grasp a moment later, she reached into her pocket for her cell and punched in the number of her attorney back in Enid. "Be brave, be brave," she whispered as the call rang through.

"Come on, Frank, pick up. It's only seven, I know you're still there…you're always there."

Chapter 18

Tio frowned. *Women never listen. My sister wouldn't. Y mi madre, she never listened to me either—and now she's dead.*

Memories of his mother invoked bittersweet emotions in Tio. There were other memories too. Memories of a little boy standing alongside the highway each morning, trying to sell flowering cactus to the gringos, rushing past to booze and broads in Tijuana. And memories of that same little boy watching in terror as his mother struggled in the dark, with the dregs tearing off one more piece of her soul, on their way back north each night.

Making ends meet had been hard, but usually there was enough. At least until…

Tio, or, Pepe, as he was called back then, could not remember when he first felt the change. It might have been the diminishing sales, when customers began to notice the sores that never seemed to heal. More likely, though, at night, as fewer and fewer revelers chose to stop.

At first, Pepe was thankful. He sensed there was little of use in the shifty-eyed strangers and their fast cars; being too young to understand the connection between a backseat wrestling match and food in his stomach.

Tio no longer let his mind wander much past the point of boarding the bus to San Antonio, to live with his older sister and her bastard. He certainly never let it reach back to the AIDS-ravaged whore he had left behind. Of more use, were lessons he had learned since then—most important of which had been to grab whatever he wanted, and hang on.

Tio had no intention of letting *any* woman, pregnant or not, take him down; as long as there was something he could do about it.

What's the big deal anyway, he wondered. It's just a simple medical procedure, not like they'd suffer or anything.

Chapter 19

I was so young… they didn't counsel me or anything… all they wanted was my money. For the rest of my life, every time I go into a Toys 'R' Us, and see a child, I'll think 'that should be me pushing that stroller.'

—Author Unknown

Darkness had come early that day, possibly due to the storm. All afternoon, pillowy, multi-hued black and blue clouds had roiled across the sky, borne on gusts of shifting winds—winds bearing just the hint of burning fields being cleared down in old Mexico.

And with the light, had gone Amy's last excuse for ignoring her child, or more precisely, the dream of her child—the child that might have been.

Carefully balancing a drink in one hand and her stack of ersatz memories in the other, Amy cautiously entered the darkened room and flipped on the light switch with her chin.

Squinting into the sudden glare as it permeated the darkest recesses of her tomb, Amy steadied herself against the doorframe, before tottering across the floor and settling onto the rug beside her bed.

"Damn," she complained, when the drink in her hand sloshed over its rim—running in cool rivulets down her fingers and into her upturned palm. Reacting quickly, she slid the half-empty glass across her nightstand, and wiped the sticky remnants of errant liquid into the thirsty fabric of her jeans.

Leaning sideways, Amy fought back against the dizzying effects of her drink, as she removed the large storage box that had gathered dust under her bed for much of the past year.

Gently wiping it's surface, she removed the more obvious evidence of her neglect, before reaching inside for the familiar stack of cards, the child's quilt and the scrapbook—all things which weighed heavily on her mind.

Spreading the delicate quilt over her lap, Amy ran her hands across it—caressing it—as if conjuring up an illusion of life, before leaning back against her bed to read each card according to its time. After adding her latest token, purchased earlier that day, Amy returned the collection to the crypt from whence they had come.

Unable to evade further her mournful fate, Amy picked up the ornately decorated scrapbook. Opening the front pocket, she carefully removed the wrinkled sonogram and placed it gently on the floor beside her. As she scanned the remaining pages of the book, Amy lovingly ran her fingers over the pictures of children she had clipped from various sources over time. There were boys and girls, blondes and brunettes. There were babies and toddlers, puppies and toys. So much, it seemed, for one heart to endure. Finally, mercifully, her endeavor reached an empty page, as it seemed had her life. Wiping a tear, Amy consecrated a new icon to the secret cache she had kept through the years.

Her onerous task complete, Amy picked up the sonogram, climbed unsteadily onto the bed, and reached for the almost forgotten glass at her side. Propping the graphic memory against an adjoining pillow, Amy wrapped the quilt around her shoulders and spread her emotion-drained corpse across the bed.

Staring at the indistinct visage beside her, Amy whispered "Happy Birthday," before turning the image once again to read the poem she had penned some years before, in a fleeting moment of inspiration.

I close my eyes and dream of you, and falls a tear like morning's dew.
To fall and die no one to hear, yet to my dreams its message clear.
I know that soon I must awake, and stay my tears for both our sake.
Yet knowing you will not be there, makes each new day so much to bear.

Sometime during the night, Amy stirred, pulling the quilt close about her, as a cold specter of death clawed silently across her heart.

Chapter 20

It is a poverty, to decide that a child must die so that you may live as you wish.

—Mother Teresa

Sarah pushed through the rusted parking garage door and cringed. The entire string of lights along the far wall was out, placing several cars, hers included, in an uncomfortable gloom.

I hate my spot, she thought, pulling her coat tight against the wind. It's always dark, and too close to the street. Sarah shuddered, remembering times she had seen vagrants seeking shelter from the cold, or, like tonight, the rain.

Maybe I'll start using one of the close-in handicap spots, she thought. The super won't mind.

Sarah reached into her purse and retrieved her keys, then, almost by instinct, poked the sharpest key between her fingers like a knife. Her mother had taught her that technique, long before she had really understood why.

Sarah pressed the remote to unlock her door. As she reached for the handle, however, a sharp blow to her wrist sent her makeshift weapon skidding across the floor.

What did I miss? Her mind raced through the last few moments. A footstep? What? It was useless now to wonder.

A second blow left her spread-eagled, facedown across the hood, a crushing weight pressing against her.

"Don't scream or I'll kill you…understand?"

Sarah remembered the life within her. She would have to endure the rape, whatever this monster wanted.

At her nod, the pressure eased, and a hand slipped between the warmth of her breasts and the cold steel of the car. Then, without pausing, it moved down.

He's in a hurry, she thought. Maybe I can hold it together if he's fast.

The hand slid down her belly, kneading her flesh as if it were bread, until, at her waist, it withdrew.

Oh, God, he knows! Maybe now he'll let me go.

Hope turned to horror, however, when the crushing weight returned.

"I thought so," he snarled.

Her mind struggled to focus. *That voice, Tio's voice!* Sarah again tried to force her body away from the car. Twisting beneath him, she lunged for his eyes with her nails.

The final blow to her pelvis ended her resistance. Resolve gone, her struggle over, Sarah slipped from his grasp as blood mixed with urine seeped into her hose.

"Damn," Amy spat, dropping heavily into her chair, "It's happened again!"

Kat spun to face her. "What?"

"Another attack. This company's fucking dangerous."

"You think it has something to do with Southwestern?"

"This is the second or third since I've been here, and all the victims leave. What's that tell you?"

"Who was it this time?"

"Sarah, for God's sake! She's so sweet. Who'd want to hurt her?"

With Maria's tragic history smoldering in the back of her mind, Kat asked, "Did she recognize him?"

"No, yes, I don't know…maybe, but she's not talking. She's really scared."

"Was she raped?"

"It's weird, evidently not. I don't even think he took her purse."

"Then what on earth did he want?"

"I don't know, but she lost her baby."

"Oh God! She was pregnant? Oh God!" Kat trembled, as Tio's conversation in the men's room came rushing back. "Where does Sarah work? What department?"

"Accounting I think. Why?"

Chapter 21

On the first Monday in September, the Employee Relations Supervisor ran across Kat's entry in her tickler file.

Oh my! She thought. It's almost time for her to leave. I'd better get busy if we're going to take up a collection and have that baby shower. I do hope a week's enough time to get everything done. I just wish she had let me put that notice in the newsletter; it certainly would've made things easier. I guess she had her reasons though, poor dear.

Come to think of it, I wonder what ever happened about that problem with her young man. Goodness, I shouldn't have let that go so long. Oh well, at least she'll be safe on maternity leave, and I'll have a chance to look into it. Satisfied with her plan, the supervisor slipped the gift envelope into the company mail.

"Tag, you're it!" the messenger said, dropping the envelope onto Tio's desk.

Lazily looking up from his work, Tio asked, "Who is it this time?"

"Oh, some snatch over in Analysis. Seems she got herself knocked up by Santa, and the girls there think that's worthy of a celebration. Actually, I thought you might know her, cuz I hear she's hot!"

Tio tightened the grip on his pen. It couldn't be, he thought. I scared the shit outa her. Only a complete idiot would've ignored that warning. Still…"What's her name?" he cautiously asked.

"I don't know for sure, Karen something or other. Anyway, it's on the envelope."

"Karen?" Tio relaxed. "I don't think I know her."

"That's pretty surprising. I thought you'd been under every skirt in the building, especially one on a green-eyed stunner like this babe."

"Shit!" Tio erupted, picking up the envelope and searching for the name. *Kar…no, Katherine*—"Katherine (Kat) Reed: Analyst, Southwestern Life Insurance Company."

There it was, right before his eyes. "*Shit!*"

"*Leave the envelope…need to get some change. I'll pass it down the line.*"

"Okay, but don't keep it too long. The party's next Monday and the super will be all over my ass if the money gets pigeon-holed."

"Don't worry, I'm gonna give this very special attention."

The messenger was barely through the door before Tio spun around and accessed the HMO database on his PC.

"*Reed, Katherine Reed*—come on you slow piece of shit," Tio grumbled, while the computer cranked through its voluminous files.

"Gotcha!" he exclaimed, when Kat's file flashed onto the screen. "Address, phone number…everything's here."

"Okay, Kitty Kat," he murmured. "Let's party!"

Chapter 22

Kat was frightened. There really wasn't much she could do about it, however, as the supervisor gleefully ushered her into the cafeteria. Not even her trusted Amy had leaked a word about the shower. It had been a complete surprise, as was the number of attendees. Kat had no idea so many people even knew her, let alone cared enough to come.

Searching frantically through the faces in the crowd, she looked for Tio, but thankfully, he was not there. Slowly, as her nerves settled, Kat began to enjoy herself. She had been under such terrific stress for so long, that she had almost forgotten how to laugh. Nevertheless, laugh she did, especially as everyone ooh'd and aah'd over the precious baby gifts.

Kat was having so much fun, in fact, she failed to notice when Tio slipped into the room, and, nodding at Amy, walked over to her. "Hi, Aim. What's shakin'?"

"Well, if it isn't Mister-T himself. How've you been? Rotten I hope."

"Aw come-on, Amy, you know it's been over between us for years. Get a life! Anyway, who's the babe?"

"Her name's 'Kat'. But relax, stud, she's leaving in a couple of days, for, as I'm sure you've noticed, she's nesting."

"Oh yeah, I've noticed," Tio replied, malice thick in his voice.

"Tio!" Amy bristled, a sudden chill creeping up her spine. "Do you know her?"

His jaw muscles twitching, Tio merely turned and walked away.

"Oh No," Amy gasped, realization flooding over her. "Oh Dear God, No!"

The girls had been dreading a visit from Tio since Amy confronted Kat after the shower and demanded to know if he was the father. When she hesitantly admitted he was, Amy began to cry. Talking through her tears, Amy told Kat, Tio had been the one who had forced her into the abortion years before. "Oh Kat, I'm so sorry. If only I'd been brave enough to tell the supervisor, that bastard would've been fired long ago, and you'd be safe."

When Tio-the-Spider did show up later that afternoon, Maria cautiously opened the apartment door.

"Where's Kat?" he demanded.

"What cat?" Maria fired back in her most convincing ethnic slang. "I ain't got no cat."

"Very funny. What're you doing in Kat's apartment?"

"I already tole you asshole, dare ain't no cats here. Now, do I need to have my man come splain it to you?"

Tio was puzzled. Unless the file was somehow out of date, he had to be at the right address. "I'm looking for an old girlfriend. You lived here long?"

"Couple years. Are we done? I got ironing to do."

Tio turned to leave. A couple of years, he thought. The file must be wrong.

"Jerk," Maria muttered, slamming the door. "So that was the infamous Tio, he didn't look so tough to me."

"Don't underestimate him," Kat warned from her hiding place. "He's as evil as they come."

"I know," Maria said. "I'll be careful."

The narrow escape with Tio had unnerved the girls more than they cared to admit. As a result, Maria spent much of the evening immersed in thought, until…

"Kat, we need to get outa here. If Tio starts checking around and finds we've tricked him, he'll be back."

"We can't just pick up and leave. I've got a lease, and there's all this stuff."

"We don't have to leave for good. All we need is to disappear till the baby's born. After that, it'll be safe to come back."

"Why would we be safe then?" Kat asked.

"If anything was to happen now, Tio might be able to convince a jury you went along with killing the baby. After it's born, he knows it would be murder no matter who agreed."

"But where can we go? You gave up your room when you moved in here, didn't you?"

"Yeah, but that wouldn't have worked anyway. We need to be where we'll have some protection around. We need to go home to Bandera."

"What makes you think Tio won't try to get to us there?"

"First of all, Tio doesn't know anything about Bandera. And even if he did, he wouldn't dare try to hurt you there. In my culture, men do horrible things to each other when a pregnant woman is hurt. Tio knows that. Don't worry; we'll be safe."

"What about your parents?" Kat asked.

"They won't care. We can bunk together in my old room. It'll be fun. You'll see."

"Sounds fine, but what about work?"

"I can commute like I did when I first got my job, and you're scheduled to go on maternity leave in a few days. Can't you just take vacation or something till then?"

"I guess so, but I'll still have to go in on Friday to sign my insurance forms."

"I wish you'd forget all that till after the baby?"

"No, it's very important, and it has to be done in person for the insurance to be effective. Maybe I can get Amy to set things up so I can sneak in and out without too much fuss."

"I still don't like it, but I guess it'll work as long as it's only the one night."

"What about tonight?" Kat asked.

"We should be fine," Maria said. "Tio won't be able to do any serious checking till he gets into the office in the morning. We'll be long gone by then."

"Oh, Maria, that sounds wonderful!"

"Well, except for having to evade Chuy," she agreed, "I think everything will work out just fine."

"Oh, goodie," Kat teased. "We're going to Bandera to seduce cousin Chuy."

"You better be good, Kat, or I'll never take you anywhere again."

"You're an old poo."

"You'll think old poo when you meet Chuy. Whatever you do, keep a firm grip on your virtue around him."

Kat patted her swollen belly and laughed. "What virtue?"

Sitting in his office the next morning, Tio wondered how Kat's file could have been so out of date. He knew it would have been checked each time she made a claim. She must have seen a doctor sometime, he thought, at least for pre-natal care. Search as he might, however, Tio was unable to find a recent entry. Leaning back with his hands locked behind his head, he realized Kat must have known she was in danger and was actively avoiding him. "There's more than one way to skin a Kat," he grumbled, turning again to his computer. "'Maternity Leave,' now that's a form she couldn't ignore." Clicking through the recent submissions, Tio quickly found what he was looking for.

"Maternity Leave Request—

"Mother: Katherine (Kat) Reed

"Father: Not listed"

Well, he thought, at least she did something right.

"Jesus!" he exclaimed, scanning the rest of the form. "It's the same address. So who the hell was that at the door?"

"Emergency contact: Maria Vargas (roommate)"

"Why that little *Chicana* bitch!" Tio said, leaning back with a self-satisfied grin.

Later that evening, Tio dialed the girls' number and waited for the answering machine to pick up. He smiled once again as he listened to the automatic greeting: "You've reached the residence of Kat and Maria. We're not home right now, so please leave a message at the tone." Tio was sorely tempted to leave the girls something to think about, but knew patience was more useful to his purpose. "They'll get the message soon enough," he muttered. "I can wait."

Chapter 23

"Jesus, Mom," Maria complained, as the screen door slammed for the umpteenth time. "Did you have to tell everyone in town we were coming?"

"Don't talk that way about Jesus, young lady," her mother scolded from the kitchen. "Besides, it's only Chuy."

"Hi, Scarface," Chuy said with a nod to Maria; then, gazing intently into Kat's startled eyes, "Lord!"

"Screw you, Chewbacca," Maria hissed. "Keep your paws off her, or I'll take away your birthday."

"Now, now children, play nice," Kat, chided, as the cousins glared at one another.

"Who told you we were here?" Maria demanded.

"You know our mothers have been scheming to get me hitched for years. As soon as my old lady heard you were here with this green-eyed beauty, her wheels spun up big time. I have to admit though," Chuy added, with a wink to Kat, "her enthusiasm has waned somewhat, since she heard you were so 'humongous with child.' But frankly," he said with a smile, "it doesn't bother me in the least."

Maria turned to Kat. "See, I told you he was a whore."

"What brings you back here?" Chuy asked, ignoring Maria's condescension.

"We're like the Blues Brothers," Kat said, "on a mission from God."

"Excuse me?"

"Forget it," Maria interrupted. "Kat doesn't have anyone to help her during the delivery, so I thought we'd move in here till she has the baby."

"Cool. We'll have plenty of time to get to know each other."

"Your ass," Maria spat. "You stay away from her."

As Kat turned to glare at Maria, Chuy raised an eyebrow.

"Well," he muttered. "I do believe the lady's interested."

Chuy was not the only one to visit that evening. Once again, Maria's extended family flocked to see her, or, maybe this time, to see the green-eyed stranger. Regardless, Kat watched from the side as Maria drew the children to her, hugged them and made them laugh. Maria will make a wonderful mother, she thought. I may not survive, but at least Baby will be fine.

Maria was exercising in the garage when Kat walked in and asked, "What the hell are you doing?"

"I'm getting ready for whatever God has planned for me."

"Well, aren't you the little bad ass," Kat said, realizing for the first time how fit Maria looked. "How long have you been doing this?"

"About a year I guess, at least since…"

"What on earth for?"

"God warned me things could get rough before this is over, and I intend to be ready."

"So, you think lifting weights and jumping around will help?"

"That and some nastier stuff I learned in self-defense class."

"You're really serious about this 'mission' thing aren't you?" Kat asked. "I just thought this was your way of dealing with all the shit that's happened to you, but you really believe you're part of some divine plan." Softening, Kat continued, "You know of course, this makes you look like a religious wacko."

"I don't care," Maria said in a solemn voice. "I just know what I believe."

"So, if I get into trouble, I just call Wonder Woman, is that it?" Then, concern clouding her eyes. "You still think Tio might get to me?"

"Not if I can help it."

"Maria, this is just crazy. You can't be serious about messing with someone like Tio."

"Oh, I'm serious all right."

"But you could get hurt, bad."

"I know."

"And yet you're still determined to fight him?"

"If I have to."

"And you're not afraid?"

"Of course I'm afraid."

Saddened by Maria's admission, Kat leaned against the doorframe and thought for a moment. "If he does hurt me Maria, you have to promise me something. Promise me you won't let some doctor kill my baby just to save me. If it can be saved, then that's what I want. Please don't let me wake up without the baby. I wouldn't want to live knowing its life was taken for mine."

"But won't you be giving up your life for it?"

"Maybe, but that's my choice."

"Damn you, Kat. You're asking an awful lot—you know how much I love you."

"If I wasn't absolutely convinced of that, I'd never trust you with the baby. Now promise me, please."

"All right, Kat," Maria sighed, "I promise, but let's pray it never comes to that."

"While we're at it, there's one more thing."

"Oh come on, Kat, you're beginning to depress the shit outa me."

"That's two more things. Your mouth is getting as gross as mine is. I think we should try not cussing around the baby."

"You're right, for the baby's sake, we should try. Now, what was the 'other' other thing?"

"If anything happens to me—"

"Oh crap, here we go again."

"Maria, stop—this is serious."

Maria wiped the sweat from her forehead. "All right, *Mamacita*, go on and get it over with. I'll be good."

"If anything happens to me, I want you to inherit all my stuff. I called my lawyer in Enid some time back and got things set up. There's my will and some trust funds from my grandparents, and my car and life insurance—I want you to have it all."

A stricken look came over Maria. "Isn't there some relative or charity you'd rather give it to?" she asked softly.

"No, there's no one else, except you and…If this baby survives, I want it to have something that was mine, something of me, something more than just a damn ceramic angel. The only way I can guarantee that, is to put you in charge. Otherwise, the government will get involved and fuck…I mean mess everything up."

"Oh and one more thing…"

"Jesus, Kat!"

"I know, I know, but this really is the last thing. If I don't make it, don't tell the baby about me until it's older—if ever. I don't want it trying to split its heart between us. You'll be its mother, and that'll be the end of it."

"Is that all, Kat?" Maria asked sadly. "Because I don't think I like you anymore."

Chapter 24

"*Jesus Cristo!*" Imelda shrieked, when she recognized Maria exiting the strange car that had just pulled into her driveway. Dropping her book, she flew off the porch and into Maria's arms, then, noticing Kat's fair complexion, stepped back with a questioning look. "*Y quién es la gringa?*"

"*Ella es mi hermana,*" Maria said, pushing Kat toward Imelda.

Imelda glared at Kat and continued, "*Una gringa hermana, que interesante.*"

"*Si,*" Maria answered, "and she's as dear to me as you are."

Imelda hesitated but a moment, before offering her hands to Kat. "Then she's dear to me as well."

Kat rolled her eyes and exhaled deeply. Then, taking Imelda's hands in her own, said, "I'm so glad to finally meet you. Maria brags about you all the time. Is it true you can walk on water?"

Laughing, the girls sought the shade of Imelda's broad veranda.

"Oh, Maria, it's been so long," she gushed. "How've you been?"

"Fine," Maria replied, "but I've missed you terribly."

"I've missed you too, *Chica*. I was hoping you'd come to graduation, everyone asked about you."

Maria ran her fingers over her scarred cheek. "I'm sorry. I just thought it best we leave things as they are, at least for now."

"You can't go on hiding from people like this," Imelda said, removing Maria's hand. "It's retarded."

"What are you gonna do now?" Maria asked, changing the subject.

"Continue with school, I guess. It seems to be the only sure way to escape this rat hole."

"Have you applied anywhere yet?" Kat asked. "I have some connections in Tulsa."

"That's sweet, but no thanks. I think I'll feel safer staying close to home—at least for the first few years. Anyway, I'm signed up for UT Austin in the spring, so keep your fingers crossed."

"You're kidding," Maria, gasped. "How the hell do you expect to afford that place?"

"I have some grants and a student loan, but I don't know about the rest. I have to do something though; I can't just lay around here the rest of my life."

Kat smiled. "That's the spirit."

"*Que onda* guys? What brings you back to beautiful Bandera? Just slumming I hope?"

"We're trying to evade a bit of a mess back in San Antonio," Kat innocently answered.

"*Chinga mija*," Imelda erupted, whipping her head toward Maria. "Are you in trouble *again*?"

"Chill out Imelda, God," Maria said. "It's not me this time; at least not directly. If you must know, Kat's got some Tasmanian devil after her, and I just thought it best we stay at my parents' till things blow over."

"So, playing like a Christian?" Imelda asked.

"Something like that," Maria answered.

"Actually it's more like a mission," Kat offered, trying to deflect Imelda's heat.

"A mission?" Imelda glared at Maria. "Like from God?"

Maria grimaced. "You two visit," she squeaked, rising to escape the impending storm, "I have to pee."

As the screen door slammed shut behind Maria, Imelda turned to Kat. "Thank God you're here; I've been so worried."

"Worried? Why?" Kat asked.

"How much has Maria told you about what happened last year?"

"You mean the rape?"

"Yeah, among other things."

"Other things? What other things?"

As Imelda paused, rethinking the wisdom of what she was about to reveal, Kat continued. "She said she'd been raped and got pregnant from it, and then something about an abortion."

"The abortion—did she tell you she did it herself?"

"No, I just thought…"

"What else has she told, or not told you?"

"That's about it I guess—is there more?"

"She never said anything about trying to kill herself?"

"Shit no, what are you talking about?"

"The baby was gonna die, she couldn't carry it to term after what that bastard did to her. Anyway, she gets it into her head to take this pill—which she tricked my uncle into giving her, I might add—so she could go to heaven and be with her *precious* Juan. She somehow figured God would accept her, since she wasn't actually committing suicide—ignoring the fact she was murdering her own baby to get there, of course."

"That's a pretty harsh way to put it, Imelda."

"Her words, not mine."

"Oh, God," Kat gasped.

"Things didn't work out exactly as she planned. There was some kind of major scene in Nuevo Laredo; I don't know all the particulars. In the end though, she obviously survived, but without the baby."

"Oh, poor Maria."

"Poor Maria, my ass, I'm just getting started."

"Go on," Kat whispered.

"Having blown her thinly veiled suicide attempt, she decides to try a more direct route—actually several at once. There's nothing shy about our little lunatic."

"So much for her free ticket to heaven."

"Yeah, well, one night she gets into her father's whisky and mixes it with some pain pills she got from God-knows-where, and tries to swallow the whole mess. Thinking *that* might not be enough, she also slit her wrist."

"Jesus, how'd she survive all that?"

"See, that's where this 'Mission from God' *mierda* comes from. She figures the only way she could have screwed everything up so bad and still survived, was if she was somehow working for God."

"You make her sound like a walking death wish."

"Maybe, maybe not. I guess it all depends on the strength of one's faith. Anyway," Imelda continued, "it's more faith than I've got at the moment, so I need your help."

"I'll do anything," Kat offered.

"Even if it means protecting Maria from herself?"

"If need be," Kat answered slowly.

"Good, because it may come to that."

"What do you mean?"

"Well, she's obviously fine right now while she thinks she's on this dumb mission, but I'm concerned if things blow up in her face, she might try it again."

"Might try to kill herself you mean?"

"Yes, that's what's been driving me crazy. Half the time I'm wondering *how* she's doing and the other half *what* she's doing. I can't watch her every move from Bandera, so you've just got to help."

"I'll do whatever I can," Kat repeated, "I promise."

"Uh-oh," Maria groaned, stepping through the door. "I knew I shouldn't have left you two schemers alone. What's up?"

"*Nada.* We're just deciding how best to hurt you for not warning me you were coming."

It seemed like hours before the girls were able to extricate themselves from Imelda's clutches and drive back across town toward home. When they crossed the Medina River, Kat noticed the park, as, it seemed, did Maria. "Is that where it happened?" Kat asked gently. Maria merely nodded and drove on.

"For a moment there, I thought Imelda was going to rip my head off," Kat said changing the subject. "What was all that Spanish stuff anyway?"

"Nothing much. Imelda just wondered who you were."

"And...?"

"I told her you were my sister, and she found that interesting."

"Interesting, why?"

"She said having a white retard in the family explained a lot."

"Thank you very much. Was that all?"

"Well, she did want to know if you had a good heart."

"A good heart? What'd you tell her?"

"I said no, of course."

"Maria, you're such a mess. I like Imelda by the way. It's obvious she cares about you, and that pleases me."

"Oh you poor misguided soul," Maria said, as they pulled into her driveway.

Later, feeling very pregnant, Kat dropped into the designated fat-lady chair, just as Maria stormed into the room. "We're in a world of shit now."

"What's wrong?" Kat asked, realizing her respite was not to be, "is it Tio?"

"Worse, my Mom says I have to go to Mass."

Kat smiled. "What's so bad about that? It'll probably do you good."

"I'm glad you feel that way, white meat, cuz you're going with me."

"Oh Maria, I can't go, I'm not Catholic."

"I don't care if you're Buddhist; I'm not gonna face that priest alone."

"I'll probably embarrass you." Kat frowned. "I don't know the first thing about how to act."

"Not to worry, *Muchacha,* just do as I do and you'll be fine."

The girls entered the church and headed for an empty pew near the back. Once again, Maria reminded Kat to behave. Kat promised to try, but the service had barely begun before Maria noticed her fidgeting by her side.

"What's the matter with you? Can't you sit still?"

"I'm sorry, but I don't understand a word he's saying, and it's scary in here. Do you really get anything out of all this?"

"I...I used to find the rituals comforting."

"Comforting, huh? There's very little I find comforting in here. For example, what are those spooky little doors over there along the wall?"

"That's where we'll be going in a few minutes to confess our sins."

"We? You mean I have to go in there too?"

"I'm only kidding," Maria said with a smile. "If they ever found a Protestant trying to sneak in there, they'd probably fumigate the place."

"You definitely need professional help. Maybe an hour or two in there *would* do you some good."

Maria frowned. "Not just yet," she said, "perhaps someday."

Kat reached over and patted her hand.

Later, as everyone around them rose and headed to the altar for Holy Communion, Maria hesitated.

"Aren't you supposed to go too?" Kat asked.

Maria lowered her eyes and sighed. "I'm not sure I'm still allowed, after what I did to my baby."

As if fate were listening, the priest called to Maria as the girls exited the church. "Oh Christ, I'm in for it now," she groaned. "I knew we shouldn't have come here tonight."

"Do you want me to head him off?" Kat offered.

"No, it's all right; I'll have to face the music eventually."

Kat stood aside as the priest took Maria's hand and quietly talked with her for a few moments. Finally, he turned, and with Maria dutifully trailing behind, reentered the church. Kat watched, ready to pounce if she detected a smidgeon of distress. To her great relief, however, they proceeded straight to the altar, where, kneeling reverently, Maria received her long-delayed absolution.

"What was that all about?" Kat asked, as they walked home from the service.

"Seems God hasn't given up on me after all."

"What do you mean?"

"Oh nothing. Anyway, the priest thinks I'm square with God, so I guess I am. Funny thing though, I kinda got the feeling he was more concerned for himself than for me."

"You think this may have something to do with your mission from God stuff?"

"I can't imagine how he'd know anything about that," Maria answered thoughtfully. "But, it certainly is strange."

Chapter 25

To understand your parents' love, you must raise children yourself.
—Chinese Proverb

Kat smiled when Chuy showed up after church. "Kind of relentless isn't he?" she observed.

"I told you he could smell a pair of panties a mile off."

"I think he's hot," Kat sighed, as Maria pulled her away from the window.

"Behave yourself," she scolded, slamming the door and pressing her back against its frame. "That's no way for an expectant mother to act."

"I'm pregnant, Maria, not dead."

"What the hell do you want?" Maria demanded as Chuy shoved his way into the house.

"I just came to offer Kat, a taste of our fair hovel's delights."

"You're full of crap," Maria hissed. "The only delights you're interested in are under her skirt."

Ignoring Maria, Chuy continued. "How about it, Kat? What would you say to some time away from Mother Inferior here, say dinner tonight?"

"Why, Mr. Chuy sah," Kat said coyly. "This is so sudden. Are you sure you want to be seen with a 'scarlet' woman? There *is* your reputation to consider, afta all."

"Are you kidding? Being seen with you'll probably get me elected mayor."

"Kat, be careful," Maria urged.

"Oh, give it a rest; he's only being nice."

"I did my best, Lord," Maria said, storming out of the room.

"How'd you like a little Mexican?" Chuy asked when he picked up Kat later that evening.

Kat smiled shamelessly. "Actually, I was kinda hoping for a big one."

"You're bad," he said with a laugh. "Seriously though, there's not much variety in Bandera, but we do make some mean Tex-Mex."

"Mexican's fine," Kat said, still enjoying the success of her joke.

The restaurant's lights were seductively low as Kat and Chuy navigated the aroma-rich atmosphere toward a dangerously discrete booth overlooking the Medina.

How many women has he beguiled in here, she wondered. Then, taking his arm, she carefully lowered her pregnant self onto the seat. *Plenty, I'd imagine.*

"I come here a lot," Chuy began, confirming her suspicion, "but you may have already heard that."

Kat laughed. "Let's just say, Stud, your reputation precedes you."

"I see you *have* been listening to Maria."

"Oh, what is it with you two, anyway; why don't you get along?"

"We get along fine. I thought you knew this was just a game we've played since we were kids."

"You're joking. You guys act like you want to kill each other."

"That's just a front. The next time you get Maria alone and vulnerable, ask her what she really thinks of me."

Maybe I will, Kat mused, as the strains of a Spanish guitar reached out to them from the shadows.

As the evening progressed, Chuy seemed to notice a preoccupation within Kat. It was obvious to Kat as well, that throughout their meal; her heart had struggled with her mind over control of the agenda. On the one hand, she had to admit the exciting man at her side intrigued her. Ultimately, though, nothing would, or ever could come of it if he was just interested in another one-night-stand. On the other hand, Chuy *was* a man, and a man's point of view was what she desperately sought. As they relaxed over Dos Equis, Kat wondered if she dared discuss her concerns with him. She knew there was a risk her intent might be misunderstood, or worse, that she would somehow alienate Chuy, which she definitely did *not* want to do. Finally, clutching the tattered remnants of her courage, she broached the subject that had been at the back of her mind all evening. "Chuy, you say Maria trusts you?"

"Yeah, she used to think my dying breath belonged to her, although I imagine she's changed her mind after what that bastard did to her last year."

"That wasn't your fault and she knows it. Look, I realize Maria's special to you, but, can I depend on you to be as honest with me as you are with her?"

"What's going on?" he asked warily. "Why so serious?"

"Can I trust you?" she demanded.

Chuy paused, seeming to reflect on the implications of his answer. "I don't imagine I have much choice, since you and Maria are so tight. Just be careful you don't regret this later."

"I understand, Chuy, but there are some things I need to know, and a man like you may have the only answers I can trust."

"A man like…Just what's so important?"

Kat hesitated a moment before continuing. "I'm concerned about my future and that of our baby."

"*Our* baby?"

"Relax stud—Maria and I share the bambino. Anyway, do you think a man would be willing to marry a woman with…with someone else's child and be able to love it as his own?"

"So that's what's been bothering you? Listen; people around here deal with that every day. If we weren't able to accept life as we found it, nobody here would ever get laid."

"Be serious," Kat said, playfully slugging his arm.

"I am serious. Now, what else do you want to know?"

"If I wasn't lucky enough to find such a man, do you think I could raise the child on my own?"

"Not *the* child, *our* child. As you said, you'd still have Maria's help. Besides, love is all that really matters."

"I think I'm beginning to understand why Maria thinks so highly of you…in her weaker moments of course."

"Any more questions smart ass?"

"Just a couple; you're not in a hurry are you? Got another date?"

"Well," he said with a smile, "I did have this cute little *Chicana* lined up just in case you didn't work out."

Kat ignored his implication. "I understand about the love, but isn't being raised in childcare a terrible fate? After all, I'd have to work."

"Childcare's a tough one. All I can say is that even though my Mother remembers how crappy she felt dropping me off, I remember how great it felt when she picked me up."

"You were in childcare?"

"Are you kidding? Lots of people in Bandera use childcare; it's almost a part of our culture."

"How does your culture feel about adoption?"

"We usually just pass kids around within the family. At least that way we know the child's loved."

"I don't know," she continued thoughtfully. "I still shudder when thinking about my baby with a stranger. In fact, I wonder sometimes if I could bear it."

"Well then, just don't let it happen."

"You make it sound so easy, but we both know it isn't. Finding the right man I mean."

"I never said it'd be easy, now, how about another beer?"

"No thanks." Kat shifted uncomfortably in her seat. "It's really not good for the baby."

"Here, let me help," Chuy said, folding his leather jacket and slipping it behind her back.

"Oh God," Kat murmured, as Chuy's influence descended over her like a veil. "Why does this always happen to me?"

"Excuse me?" he asked.

"It's nothing. By the way, is this the normal seduction package or something special?"

Chuy leaned back in his chair and smiled. "Am I embarrassing you?"

"Well, considering your reputation…" Then, "Speaking of reputation, how is it you haven't married?"

"I guess my problem's been expectations," Chuy began. "Maria calls them unreasonable expectations."

"Oh, poor baby," she said sarcastically. "You know what they say about women and expectations don't you?"

"What?"

"If a woman doesn't meet your expectations…"

"Yes? …," he asked.

"Lower your expectations."

As a smile slowly spread across his face, Chuy fired back. "Maybe after tonight I won't have to."

"You devil," she said. "Don't you dare pull that shit with me!"

"What about you," Chuy asked, "haven't you ever been in love?"

"I've been in love thousands of times, if only in my dreams. That's the problem. I keep falling so easily, I'm afraid to trust my emotions anymore."

"What about your instincts?"

"I'll answer that later."

"So, is there anything else you want to know?"

"No, that's about it I guess, except…" She paused. "I wonder what woman would *ever* be right for you."

"What you really want to know," he said with a laugh, "is if that woman were you."

"No, I didn't mean…," she stammered, thoroughly embarrassed.

Chuy hugged her and grinned. "It's all right. I was just teasing."

Twisting out of his grip, she smiled. "You *are* a devil!"

"Now it's my turn," he said, becoming serious again. "What's all this about some guy bothering you back in San Antonio?"

"Nothing much," she lied. "It just seems the father and I have differing opinions as to what to do about the baby."

"You're kidding, as far along as you are?"

"Yeah. Anyway, Maria thought it best we come here until after the momentous event."

"Safer, you mean."

Unable to respond, Kat lowered her eyes.

"One thing I don't understand," Chuy persisted. "If this guy's such a bastard, why'd you ever hook up with him in the first place?"

"Stupidity I guess," Kat replied, seeking an end to his inquisition, "or loneliness. After a while, it kinda warps your judgment. Still, I should've known…"

"We'd better go, or we'll be late," Chuy whispered, sparing her further embarrassment.

"Late? For what?"

"Oh you're gonna love this."

"Tell me," she demanded.

Chuy smiled. "If I told you, it wouldn't be a surprise."

"Maria warned me about your surprises."

True to form, Chuy's 'surprise' dealt with love and lust…in Spanish!

"Chuy," Kat grumbled, as the lights went down in the theater, "you know I won't understand this."

"*Su corazón*...your heart will," was his only reply.

While the intensely passionate tale played itself out, Kat, as expected, became entranced. When, during one particularly moving scene, Chuy felt her shudder by his side, he reached out and placed his hand over hers, then, somehow forgot to remove it. Several moments passed before Kat, looking down, somehow forgot to remind him. Later, as she retrieved yet another tissue from her purse, Kat realized how much she had missed the joy of a good man's company. Suddenly feeling very alone, she moved closer to Chuy and laid her head against his shoulder. In a motion so natural as to almost go unnoticed, he bent and kissed her hair.

Time passed and the movie played on, but neither of them noticed, nor cared.

> September 12: Dear Diary
>
> What a disaster! I warned her and did my best to keep them apart, but guess what? Kat and Chuy are out on a date, doing God knows what. I swear, once she got a look at him, it was like talking to the wall. She drives me nuts. One minute she's worried the sky's about to fall, and the next, she's throwing her pregnant self at the worst womanizer in Bandera County. I feel like popping her sometimes.
>
> Lord, give me strength!

Later that evening, much too late as far as Maria was concerned, she finally heard Chuy's Porsche roar down the street. Her relief was short-lived, however, as the two-and-a-half most important people in her life remained sitting, too close for too long in the dark. Beside herself, Maria flipped on the porch light and growled in frustration when the couple finally strolled up the path.

Realizing they were not alone, Chuy pulled Kat into the shadows out of Maria's view. Gently placing his hand on her belly, he leaned forward and kissed her. As she yielded her lips to the demands of her heart, time stopped for Kat—but not for Maria.

"Go home!" she yelled, pushing Chuy out of the way and pulling the reluctant mother-to-be through the open door. "Don't you ever listen?" she screamed at Kat. "That man's a sleaze!"

Kat struggled to escape the lingering power of Chuy's embrace. Then, taking Maria by the shoulders, she asked the question that had lain heavily on her mind for much of the evening. "Maria, please, *tell me the truth*. Do you trust Chuy?" Feeling Maria stiffen, Kat continued, "I must know. The fate of our baby may depend on your answer."

Slowly, as if painfully choosing her words, Maria lowered her eyes and began, "Chuy is capable of...has done things, horrid things. He can be violent and dangerous if he has to be, but aside from a string of broken hearts, I've never known him to hurt a woman or child. He's lied, even to me, but never when asked for the truth. At the hospital in San Antonio, it was his voice, more than any other, that lulled me to sleep at night, and whose smile welcomed my eyes as I awoke the next morning. He held my spirit safe within his heart, when I would have lost it on my own. Chuy's the brother I never had, and yet, never missed, because he was always there."

"But can I trust him to tell *me* the truth?"

"If you trap him into promising you, then you can trust him. However, be very sure you can live with what you ask. One more thing—I will personally strangle you if you fall for that creep."

Kat smiled and leaned into Maria's face. "I think he's cute."

"Ugh!" Maria groaned, as Kat, seductively twitching her hips, headed for the bath. "Be sure you scrub real good this time," Maria called after her. "You're beginning to smell like a cat in heat."

While packing for their trip back to San Antonio the next morning, Maria seemed more agitated than normal. Finally, unable to contain herself further…"Kat, I need your help again."

"Certainly, what is it?"

"I want to place some flowers in the park where, you know, where my Juan was killed."

"But isn't he in a cemetery around here someplace?"

"No, his family's from Mexico, so they had him shipped there—I never even had a chance to say goodbye. All that's here is a marker."

"Do you think we can find it?" Kat asked tenderly.

"I think so," Maria answered. "I've had lots of practice searching for it in my dreams."

As the girls strolled through Bandera's park, it took Maria but a few moments to find the memorial. It wasn't much, just Juan's name and space for a future inscription. Maria lowered herself to the grass and gently brushed her fingertips over his name, as if to sear the letters permanently across her heart.

Barely breathing, Kat stood for a time apart, allowing Maria these precious few moments with her love.

Finally, wiping the remnants of a tear from her cheek, Maria rose and walked slowly into Kat's arms.

"I've needed to do this for so long," she admitted sadly, "but I just didn't have the courage to face it alone."

"I'll always be with you," Kat whispered, as they turned and walked toward home.

The girls were loading the last of their luggage as Chuy pulled into the driveway. Maria rolled her eyes in disgust, then, shook her finger at Kat, warning her to behave.

Chuy paused only long enough to slap Maria on the butt, as he headed straight for Kat.

As if by instinct, Kat reached out to touch him, to pull his lips to hers.

Turning his attention to Maria, Chuy cautioned, "You guys be careful in San Antonio."

Unable to escape as he advanced on her, Maria finally relented, giving Chuy a quick hug before again pushing him away.

"Hey, I got hugged. Things are looking up."

"I was just picking your pocket," Maria smirked, pitching him his wallet.

"Damn you're good," Chuy said, sticking his head through the open window. "Seriously though, I meant what I said. Be careful and get back here as fast as you can."

"Don't worry," Maria chimed in. "We're going to the office together. I'll look after her."

"Oh yeah, hot shot," Chuy said with a hint of sarcasm, "and just who's gonna look after you?"

"I will," Kat answered, before quickly turning to hide the fear, or was it sadness, flashing across her eyes.

"I still wish you'd call the cops on this guy."

"I can't," Kat complained. "That would be disastrous."

"Why?"

"Visitation…or even worse, custody. With parental rights on his side, he could…No; we have to do this ourselves."

"Now leave us alone, *puto*," Maria hissed, pushing him away from her window.

As she slipped the car into gear, Kat turned for one last glance at Chuy.

Maria noticed…

"So, you two have an understanding now?" she probed, as Bandera disappeared into the sunset.

"Maybe," Kat hedged, "just as long as it doesn't go to his crotch."

Later, somewhere along the road to San Antonio, Maria turned to Kat. "It's strange. The last time I was in Bandera, all I could see was darkness and death; but this time, with you, it was different."

Chapter 26

The phone rang as Kat entered their apartment. Answering without thinking, she cringed when the line went dead. "Damn, I hate that!"

"Wrong number?" Maria asked, dragging her suitcase through the open door.

"I'm not sure," Kat, answered.

"What do you mean? Didn't they say who it was?"

"No nothing, except, I thought I heard breathing on the other end of the line."

"Jesus, Kat, this could be important; check the messages."

"There's three—a couple from the same number that just hung up, and a different one from earlier this morning."

The first two messages the girls played back, as feared, were blank. The final message, however, was from Amy informing Kat that the insurance papers were ready for her signature, just as she had asked. In addition, Amy recommended she arrive early to avoid running into Tio. Then, before hanging up, she mentioned they might want to remove the outgoing message from their answering machine.

"Thanks Amy," Kat said, pushing the master erase on the recorder. "Unfortunately, it's a tad late for that now.

"Maria, I shouldn't have answered that last call."

"What do you mean?"

"I don't think those were wrong numbers after all. I think Tio may have found us. I suspect he's been calling here each evening, and now, thanks to my carelessness, he knows we're back."

"You're probably right," Maria said bitterly. "Although, we've always felt it was just a matter of time."

"But why'd it have to be *now*? Now when we're so close to being rid of him. Damn!

"Well that's it," Kat grumbled, heading for the kitchen. "No more picking up until after the baby's born. If the phone rings, we'll just let the answering machine get it…Deal?"

"Deal," Maria answered solemnly.

Later that evening, Maria noticed Kat reaching for a tissue. "Thinking about Tio again?" she asked.

"Oh, Maria, why's he doing this?"

"I don't know," Maria began. "Creatures like Tio don't seem to need a reason. I'm not even sure they realize the risk they're taking with God."

"You're such a special person, Maria. I've never told you this before, but, if it hadn't been for you, I'd probably have gone back to that abortion clinic, or at best, given the baby away to the first stranger I came across. Before we met, I was so desperate for my own life, I couldn't even think about anyone else. If this baby survives, I swear it'll owe its life to you."

"Kat, don't say that. You're its mother."

"That may be, but if it's a girl, I intend to name her 'Maria.'"

"Hey, I thought we were gonna pick the name together. I was kinda voting for 'Katherine' or 'Kathy' myself."

September 13: Dear Diary

I just checked on Kat. She's out cold, thank God. I've been worried that with all this going on, she wouldn't be able to sleep.

Guess what? I felt the baby kicking through my tummy tonight. It felt so strange. It was like...I don't know, something more than natural, almost supernatural. Kat says that since I've felt the baby kick, she—we've decided it's gotta be a girl—now truly belongs to both of us. Kat thinks there's some kind of shot I can take, oxy-something, that will make my milk come in, so we can both breastfeed her, but I don't know. That seems a bit too weird for me.

Anyway, I've been praying we get safely through the next few days. I know I should just trust in God, but I can't seem to stop worrying. I'm so afraid for Kat and the baby. If anything should happen to them, I think I'd die.

Please, Lord...Oh, see, there I go again.

It just feels like things are spinning out of control. We shouldn't be here; we should be home in Bandera with Chuy. And we certainly shouldn't be going into the office tomorrow, insurance or no insurance.

Poor Kat, this has been so hard on her—on both of us. Thank God, we have each other. When I think of what we've been through these last few months, it seems almost surreal.

Oh well, a little while longer and we can head for home.

I hope Kat remembered to set her alarm.

After struggling to keep her eyes open to finish the final line, Maria drifted into sleep, and, in a few moments, into her dream. This time, however, the dream was far different from the horror of her past. Although, like before, she was in the park and not alone, gone were the violence and her pain. In fact, she merely walked hand-in-hand with Juan through the morning mist. Not much of a dream…but it was enough.

Awakening with a start, Maria added a last few words to the diary, then, clutching it close to her breast; closed her eyes and once again stepped back into the dream.

Dawn was still hours away when Kat's alarm began to play her favorite tune. Rising, she silenced the alarm, and then quickly made her way to Maria's room. Ever since the rape,

Maria had felt safer with a small light near her bed. Standing for a moment, with Maria asleep in its glow, Kat noticed the diary. Gently sliding it from Maria's grasp, Kat guiltily read the crucial passage: "Thank you, Lord, for revealing your will to me in time. Tomorrow, I'll be with you in paradise."

Kat gasped. "Oh, no, what've you talked yourself into now?" Then, remembering Imelda's prophetic warning. "My God, she's going to try to kill herself again!"

Finally confronting the demon that had troubled her for so many months, Kat realized she could no longer endanger her sister of the heart. "Sleep on, little one," she whispered, reaching for Maria's light, "and forgive me."

Chapter 27

The automatic timer unlocked the night security gate as Kat drove up to the garage. Good, she thought, at least no one's been able to drive in ahead of me. Now if I can just get back out before they open the rest of the building.

Making her way through the dimly lit halls, Kat smiled as she remembered raising her gown and lying belly-to-belly with Maria the evening before, all in the hope that Maria would feel the baby kick, just as she had.

When Kat arrived at her desk, she found the medical insurance forms and final paycheck, as expected. There was also an envelope from Amy, emblazoned with the words "I'm Proud of You."

Kat decided to leave the card for later, slipping it unread into her purse, next to the gun she had never quite learned to use. Had she taken the extra few moments to read the card, she would have learned how pleased Amy was that she had stuck it out. She would also have read Amy's plea—not to leave without first notifying Security. But then, Kat was in a hurry.

As the elevator doors finally closed, she sighed in relief. A few more minutes and she and the baby would be safe, hopefully forever. Her constant struggle to stay focused, to keep her mind off Tio and her fear, would be over, and she could relax.

But not just yet...

The elevator slowing abruptly ended Kat's daydream. It's too soon, she thought. The parking garage is still several floors down.

Oh, God, please don't let it be...

"*Tio!*" she gasped, as the doors slid open, revealing the spider, patiently awaiting his prey.

"Hi, Kat," he said coldly. "Long time no see."

Kat backed away as she saw Tio wrapping the end of a heavy leather belt, tightly around his fist. In a panic, she desperately tried to push past him. Tio was too quick, however, catching her by the throat and slamming her head back against the elevator wall.

Stunned, Kat was unable to protect herself as Tio savagely whipped the free end of his belt across her breasts. "You asked for this."

Instinctively raising her hands to protect her throbbing breasts, Kat inadvertently provided Tio the opening he sought. Kat screamed as she felt him whip her again, this time striking her unprotected belly. As Tio's belt snapped painfully around her, she felt the baby flex within her. Instantly, she lowered her hands to protect her middle. He would not get another chance to harm her baby, no matter what she had to endure. Unable to defend herself further, she turned her back on Tio's anger, and his lash.

Finally, with her strength nearly gone, strength she would need to protect her baby, Kat cried out the words he had wanted to hear. She would do, as he demanded. To give her baby one last chance to live, she would go with him to the clinic and agree to the abortion, trusting that God, and a little luck, would decide their ultimate fate.

"How could she be so stupid as to go in alone?" Maria cried. "God, you know I'm supposed to protect her—to die for her. Now I don't even know where she is. *What is it You want from me?*"

Maria frantically picked up the phone and called Amy. "Kat's gone—have you seen her?"

"No Maria, but the insurance papers have been signed and her check's gone, so I'm sure she's been here. Maybe…," Amy added hopefully, "maybe she's just been delayed."

"Delayed? It's been hours since she left to sign those damn papers. Christ, Amy!" Maria slammed down the phone. "She could be dead by now!"

Chapter 28

Her passing is a testament to the truth that human life is a gift from God and that children are always to be fought for, even if life requires — as it did of Susan — the last full measure of devotion.

—Justin Torres on the death of his sister-in-law, Susan M. Torres

The San Antonio Family Planning Clinic was not a very comforting place to visit. In fact, one really needed a compelling reason to be there, as a patron, or, for that matter as an employee. For the resident doctor, the compelling reason was money. Originally, he had been seduced by the cause of "a woman's right to choose." Having barely survived several malpractice suits by the very individuals he sought to help, however, all vestiges of abortion rights support were long gone. Somewhere along this slippery path between ethics and economics, the doctor finally acknowledged he was just in it for the paycheck, a very good paycheck.

It had been a slow morning, which was unusual for a Friday. Normally, the clinic would be teeming with pre-weekend customers "getting it over with."

Taking advantage of the curious lull in their routine, the doctor and resident nurse were sharing a pot of coffee in the break room, when he casually asked, "So tell me, how long have you worked here?"

"About fifteen years now," the nurse answered.

"That long? And you're still sane?"

"Sometimes I'm not so sure," she said with a smile. "It's really not that bad; at least not like it used to be."

"What changed?"

"Well, when I first started here, we were doing partial-birth procedures."

"You actually did those here?"

"Yeah, back then it was tough coming to work."

"I can imagine. Why'd you stop doing them?"

"One day not too long after I came to work here, we had a horrible incident. Are you sure you wanna hear this?"

"Yeah, sounds interesting."

"It was in '93, I think, late September or early October. Anyway, we got this temp through a local employment agency."

"You used to get your nursing staff from a temp agency?"

"We had to. Like I said, back then this wasn't a very popular place to work."

"Go on."

"I guess the nurse figured she could handle the job, being pro-choice and all. Actually, she had no idea what a screwed up partial could be like."

"So, she had a bad experience?"

"We all did."

"What happened?"

"The first client we had that morning evidently lied about how far along she was in her pregnancy.

Although, I'm not really sure it would've mattered to the doctor we had at the time."

"How far along was she?"

"Far enough for the baby to somehow sense it was in danger and start fighting for its life."

The doctor sighed. "Sounds like a real nightmare."

"The baby didn't have a chance, of course. None of them do once they get this far."

"So the nurse freaked?"

"No, she went ahead and did her job, like she was supposed to. She just didn't show up for work the next day."

"Was that it?"

"Oh no, that was only the beginning. About a week later, we started getting phone calls from the media asking what had happened."

"You mean she went to the press?"

"Not directly. Evidently she was so affected she went to see a shrink. Unfortunately, someone got hold of her information and put it on the Internet."

"You're kidding!"

"No, I'm serious. In fact, her story's still there. All you have to do is enter 'what the nurse saw' in a search engine to find it. But I warn you, it's pretty gross."

"She wasn't some closet pro-lifer then?"

"Nope, just tragically naive."

"How'd that affect the clinic?"

"Well, as you can imagine, when the media got wind of the story, they were all over us like flies on shit. It got so bad, that for a while our clients wouldn't come near the place for fear of ending up on the evening news."

"What'd you do?"

"We finally had to stop doing partials, just to stay in business."

"Fortunately that's all behind us now," he said.

"Don't be so sure. We still get flakes now and again, like that bunch taking pictures a couple of weeks back. It seems they've never forgotten the damage that notoriety did to our business. In fact, I'll bet this last episode was an attempt to repeat their success."

"Come to think of it, I do remember hearing something about that nurse. So this was the clinic, huh?"

"Unfortunately, yes, and we've spent years trying to live it down."

"With all that's happened I'm surprised you're still working here."

The nurse sighed. "Someone has to look after these poor women."

"Have you ever talked with a counselor yourself?" he asked.

The nurse raised an eyebrow. "What about?"

"About what happened and how it might have affected you?"

"I'm okay. At least I still believe in miracles." Then, frowning, she added, "I just wish we could find a way to do without all this."

"Speaking of miracles, did you hear I'm writing a book?"

"Is this another of your pathetic jokes?"

"No, really, it's about repeaters. Guess what it's called?"

"I shudder to think."

"The Third Fetus of Eve"

"That's disgusting. You really are sick."

"Seriously, you realize of course that if they stop doing abortions, you'll be out of a job."

"I think I'd manage," the nurse replied, as the security buzzer announced a new arrival. "Wonder who that is?" She rose wearily. "Our first appointment isn't till noon."

"I'll be across the hall if you need me," the doctor said. "Who knows, maybe this one's your miracle."

Smiling politely, the nurse greeted the young couple as they entered the clinic. When Tio demanded an immediate abortion, however, her initial pleasantness evaporated.

"That's not our procedure. What on earth makes you think you can just walk in here and—"

"This does," Tio snarled, pulling the gun he had taken from Kat's purse in the elevator. Moving quickly, he locked the front door and hung the "CLOSED" sign before herding Kat and the nurse down the hall and into the operating room. As they entered, the doctor glanced up, fear draining the color from his face.

"All right folks," Tio began, "listen up. If you don't want to get hurt, do exactly as I say. First, relax. I won't use this gun unless you force me to. I don't want your money, and I don't want your advice. In a couple of minutes you're gonna take this baby, and tonight, everyone gets to go home like nothing ever happened."

Keep talking, asshole! Kat thought. You're out of your mind if you think I'm going to let you destroy my baby without the fight of your life. One mistake, make just one mistake.

With Tio distracted, Kat eased her hand into her purse and discreetly punched the apartment speed-dial button on her cell phone.

"Please God," she murmured, "let Maria be there."

Remembering the rules, Maria frantically waited for the answering machine to pick up the call. After what seemed like an eternity, she was shocked to hear Tio's voice in the background at the other end of the line. She realized he had taken Kat, but where? Finally, she heard a voice mention "family planning."

"Family planning, my Catholic ass," Maria muttered, grabbing her keys. "Family felony is more like it!"

As the doctor examined Kat, he noticed the welts from her beating. Turning, he confronted Tio. "How could you do such a thing?"

"Don't pull that ethics crap with me," Tio mocked. "You deal misery and death outa this room every day, so spare me the attitude."

Disgusted, the doctor turned back to Kat. "I'm going to be giving you a shot to induce your labor. It's very powerful," he explained, "so there won't be a lot of time to get ready. Once the injection takes hold, things will move quickly. You won't have to do anything except grit your teeth and hang in there. I'd normally have given you something for the pain, but there's no time now, so tell me when you feel the baby drop, and I'll give you a quick-acting local."

"Please!" Kat reached out and grabbed the doctor's arm. "If this were a normal delivery, would my baby live?"

"As far as I can tell...yes. Unfortunately, there may not be enough time for you to dilate. Even if we tried, its survival, and yours, would be totally out of my hands. I'm sorry, but under the circumstances..."

"Will the baby suffer?"

"I...I can't be sure."

"Please, don't do this!"

"I don't have a choice."

"You *have* a choice...God gave you a choice."

The doctor picked up the needle. "Look around," he said with a frown. "God doesn't work here."

It had been less than ten minutes since the call, by the time Maria arrived at the clinic and discovered the sign hanging on the door. Carefully approaching, she looked through to the empty lobby. Convinced she was at the right place, Maria ran to the side of the building where she found Kat's car parked in the alley. Racing back, she banged her fists against the door for attention.

Tio bolted to investigate the commotion. "Don't do anything stupid while I'm gone," he warned.

Kat's prayer for a mistake had apparently just been answered.

Arriving in the lobby, Tio came face to face with Maria, glaring at him through the door.

"Oh, shit!" she yelled, when Tio raised his gun and fired. Although the bullet whizzed harmlessly past, the front door showered her with glass as it exploded from the concussion. Sensing he had missed, Tio crept forward.

Suddenly, the operating room door slammed shut behind him, as Kat ran down the hall toward the alley.

Abandoning Maria, Tio turned quickly and fired a single shot.

Kat barely felt the bullet as it entered her body and shattered her spinal column. There was but a momentary bee-sting of pain, followed by a radiating sensation of heat. Certainly less than one would expect, considering the enormous damage being done. The impact of the bullet caught Kat in mid-stride, spinning her into the wall. Unable to move—unable to feel, Kat dropped to the floor.

Realizing he was shooting at Kat; Maria burst through the door and vaulted onto his back. Wrapping her arm in a chokehold around his throat, she raked the nails of her free hand across his eyes. No longer, the timid little girl from Bandera, Maria fought Tio fearlessly, and with a passion, only God's protection could provide. Tio would not be allowed to harm Kat and the baby further, while breath remained in her body.

Unable to escape Maria's death grip, Tio swung his gun, smashing her in the mouth and knocking her to the floor. Bleeding at the eyes, he turned and staggered toward the exit.

He never made it...

The full measure of God's retribution struck Tio, as—coming from behind—Maria projected her heel into the small of his back, launching him into the shattered glass door and altering his stunningly handsome face forever. Tio collapsed, as Maria stood defiantly over him, fists ready. She was still standing there when the nurse yelled, "Help me, please—your friend's been shot!"

Maria rushed down the hall to find Kat propped against the alley door—her water had broken!

"There's no time for a local," the doctor said. "Can you stand the pain?"

"Don't worry about me," Kat gasped, "whatever you do, save my baby!"

The doctor gently placed his hand on her shoulder. "We're going to save you both."

A moment later, her body flexed involuntarily as the baby entered her birth canal, and then stopped. Kat sensed something was terribly wrong.

Answering the concern in her eyes, the doctor began, "You're not ready. There's no room for—"

Kat stopped him in mid-sentence. "Please, you have to go in."

"Do you know what you're saying?" the doctor asked. "It could kill you."

"I'm probably dead already, and you know it. Now, please…save my baby!"

Faced with no other choice, the doctor quickly cut Kat's vaginal opening.

Although Kat could not feel the baby or the blade, Maria did! The flash of cold steel and searing pain exploding within her mind, transported Maria back through time and space to Bandera's park, where once again, she knelt, trembling in the presence of Death. Were it not for the power of Kat's voice tugging at her heart, Maria might never have returned from the abyss.

"Maria, look who's here," Kat rejoiced, when the doctor placed the baby in her arms. Staring in awe, Kat felt a strange certainty come over her. It was finally so clear...clear she had made the right choice, in spite of all she had suffered at the hands of—

"Tio...where's Tio?"

"Don't worry about him," Maria said with an awkward smile. "I kicked his ass."

"We're not supposed to cuss around the baby, remember?" Kat scolded gently. "And another thing..."

"Oh no," Maria groaned, "not that 'another thing' stuff again."

Kat ignored her complaint and continued. "You shouldn't have come alone. You could have been killed."

"God looks after me. Don't you remember?"

"Well," Kat said, wiping the blood from around Maria's mouth, "He needs His glasses checked."

Kat's mood suddenly turned fearful. "Doctor, I can't..."

"Lie still," he cautioned, "everything will be fine."

Suspecting he was lying, Maria turned on him, screaming. "Do something...please!"

"I'm sorry, but the bullet..."

"Maria, take the baby and go," Kat pleaded, as sirens wailed in the distance. "Don't let Tio get to her or he'll kill her like he said."

"Kat," Maria sobbed, "please don't send me away."

Her voice growing weaker, Kat persisted. "Don't be frightened little one. You must...the baby."

It was time...

Kat felt the warmth enter her in a rush of calming peace, stealing her breath, transforming her agony. She imagined herself rising and saw the light...calling to her, compelling her with its brilliance, seducing her with its love.

It was time...

"Oh, Mother of God!" As Maria stared in disbelief, her vision twisted through a seemingly endless vortex of pain. She tried to scream, but the foul odor of fear consumed her breath. Slipping away, she entered a vale of silence, devoid of all, but the erratic beat of a broken heart, until...

"Please...," the nurse pleaded. "You can't wait any longer. Take the baby and go, quickly, before the police see her."

"Police?" Maria gasped, struggling against the desolation pervading her mind. "Won't they...won't they find out about her?"

"Don't worry. They'll assume the fetus was destroyed."

"Do you think? Oh Jesus, do you think it'll work?"

"Sure it will. That's what we do around here all the time, and they know it. Besides, no one's going to sift through our trash. Now get going before word gets out that we're delivering babies instead of killing them."

"... or that God has found good, even within such evil," Maria whispered, wrapping the baby within the folds of her blouse and reaching for the alley door.

A warm summer rain gently fell as Maria stepped through the heavy steel door and out onto the landing.

"Jesus, Kat, no!" she wept, consumed by her loss.

Descending the stairs, she stumbled through the enveloping mist. Faster and faster she raced, trying to outrun her tears. Suddenly a sound...a sound so special as to be almost holy, drove her to her knees. The baby at her breast, *her* baby, had begun to cry. Slowly, carefully, Maria unwrapped the child and watched, breathless, as she moved, listened as she cried, counted her fingers and toes. "Juanito, my love," she whispered. "Look what God has given us."

The rain settled over her, as if washing her sins, cleansing her soul. Finally, Maria once again placed the baby within the folds of her blouse and walked out of darkness—into the light.

Chapter 29

Amy found it impossible to focus her mind after Maria's frantic call that morning. Each task melted into confusion at the slightest provocation. Each sound pierced her concentration like a thorn through flesh. Particularly vexing were the periodic outside phone calls with their unique ring. Just such a ring had barely begun as Amy lunged for the receiver.

"Southwes—" she began.

"Amy...she's dead!"

"Maria...thank God it's you. Dead—who's dead?"

"Kat...Kat's dead!"

A wave of devastation slammed into Amy, pitching her forward against her desk. "Oh my God, how'd it happen?"

"Tio shot her."

"That fucking lowlife bastard...Where's he now?"

"I don't know. He was still at the clinic when I left."

"Is he after you?" Amy's anger quickly turned to fear. "Are you in danger?"

"No, not from him anyway."

"How can you be sure?"

"Because I think I killed him...Amy, I had to. He was shooting at Kat."

"Honey, you have to go to the police."

"I can't. They'll take the baby."

"What are you talking about? What baby?"

"Kat's baby, she had her just before..."

"Good Lord, Maria, what are you doing?"

"I don't know what I'm doing. Oh, Amy, I'm so scared!"

"Well first things first. We have to do something about the baby. Is she all right?"

"I think so; she's asleep on my lap."

"When she wakes up, you're gonna need formula, and blankets...and some diapers. Can you get them without drawing too much attention?"

"Sure, we've lots of that stuff at the apartment."

"Good. Get everything you can cram into the car and disappear—fast!"

"Okay."

"Do you have someplace to go?"

"Bandera, I guess. No one here knows where I'm from, so it should be safe."

"Good idea. Call me when you get there—"

"Gotta go," Maria broke in.

"Maria, I mean it. Call...or at least write when you get there."

Amy sat stunned for a moment, staring at Kat's empty chair, before returning the phone to its cradle. Then, as waves of sadness washed over her, she lowered her head and wept.

Chapter 30

*... furthermore, I will not give to a woman
an instrument to produce abortion.*

—From the Hippocratic Oath, Hippocrates

The morning was wet and dreary. Remnants of the previous evening's rainsqualls, signifying the arrival of a late-season front, merely added to Dr. Herrera's already foul mood.

Deep in thought, the ancient medical examiner walked slowly down the hallway toward the Lab.

On almost any other Saturday, the doctor would be off fishing with his favorite grandson. Unfortunately, last evening's urgent call from the District Attorney could not be ignored.

According to the D.A., a Hispanic male allegedly shot and killed an Anglo female, following a medical procedure conducted under somewhat less than voluntary circumstances.

Although the available information was still rather sketchy, the D.A. felt strongly that "special," meaning "ethnically-sensitive," handling was appropriate.

Dr. Herrera slept poorly after their conversation. All too often these days, the term "medical procedure" meant "abortion"; an expedient he found increasingly difficult to accept.

Pausing at the laboratory door, he scanned the various admittance documents while rubbing the early morning chill out of his arthritic shoulder.

ADMISSION'S REPORT

> Deceased: White female—late twenties—5 feet 10 inches, 140 pounds.
> Preliminary cause of death: Gunshot—lower back—no apparent point of egress.
> General aspect: Numerous welts—chest, abdomen, back and buttocks. Surgical incision—(vaginal)—apparently related to a clinically induced abortion.

"'Abortion,' I thought so," he grumbled, pushing open the laboratory door.
Hesitating but a moment, he approached the elevated platform and pulled away the plastic sheet.

Something was clearly wrong!

Kat's body lay facedown on the examining table, an inglorious position undoubtedly chosen to allow access to the bullet's point of entry.

What initially caught the doctor's eye; however, were the welts across her back, buttocks and down her legs.

"Somebody hurt you real bad, didn't they little one?"

Dr. Herrera sighed deeply. Taking Kat's hand, he noted her professionally manicured nails and the smoothness of her skin. Conditions suggesting a life far removed from toil—if not tribulation. There was also an obvious ring indentation, although its shape seemed inappropriate for a wedding band. A quick glance at her personal effects list, confirmed a college ring.

As he continued, the doctor made a mental note to call the D.A.: Single white female, financially secure, above-average education, probably professionally employed. The D.A. was right—this death wouldn't go unnoticed.

Turning his attention to the entry wound, he realized the blood-loss notation on the admission's form was far different from the actual indications he was seeing. Where's all the blood, he wondered, while pulling a lever to unlock the table.

"Damn," he muttered, as Kat's "medical procedure" rotated into view. "It looks like those butchers may have killed another one."

Sliding film into his x-ray viewer, the doctor methodically traced the bullet's path from point of entry to its final resting place among the shattered remains of Kat's spine.

"Maybe, maybe not," he murmured, reaching for the pneumatic saw.

The day almost breathed its last by the time Dr. Herrera walked to his desk and completed the obligatory form.

AUTOPSY REPORT

AUTOPSY NO: A07–272
AUTOPSY D/T: 9/15/07@0930
NAME: REED, KATHERINE, A,
DOB: 3/01/80
DEATH D/T: 9/14/07@1023
AGE: 27Y
SEX: F
FINAL DIAGNOSIS:
    Heart failure
    Massive loss of blood
    Vaginal incision
    Spinal hemorrhage
    Gunshot wound to lower middle back
    Abrasions of middle/lower back, buttocks and posterior lower legs

Toxicologic Studies
blood ethanol—NEGATIVE
blood drug screen—POSITIVE (Prostaglandin 40 mg)

CLINICOPATHOLOGIC CORRELATION: Cause of death of this 27-year-old female is heart failure by massive loss of blood associated with gross vaginal incision.

C.E. Herrera, M.D.
Chief Pathologist—Medical Examiner
End of Report

Something's wrong here, the doctor mused. Why all the cutting? Far too much damage for a routine episiotomy. Why not do a partial-birth procedure and section the fetus? Looks more like a problematic delivery than an abortion. "The D.A.'s going to love this one."

Chapter 31

*The tragedy of life is not so much what men suffer,
but rather what they miss.*

—Thomas Carlyle

Physically and emotionally drained, Maria was sitting at the kitchen table staring into a cup of hot coffee, when the screen door suddenly flew open.

"Shit, what now?" she grumbled under her breath.

Maria leaned forward to peer through the doorway, then, almost fell out of her chair as Chuy stormed across the front room. In a futile attempt to escape his wrath, she dived under the table. Unfortunately, she barely made it out the other side, before Chuy grabbed the neck of her T-shirt and roughly flipped her onto her back. Stretched beyond endurance, the cotton fabric ripped as Maria's head bounced heavily off the floor.

"Enjoying the view?" she spat, attempting to cover her exposed breasts with the tattered remains of her shirt.

"What've you done?" Chuy yelled, holding her down.

"I haven't done anything," she screamed. "Get off me!"

"How could you let Kat go to that place alone? What were you thinking?"

Maria's head throbbed painfully. "She wanted to go alone. I begged her not to."

"Bull shit! You were supposed to…you promised you'd go with her."

"I tried! Now get the fuck off me before I kick your balls through the ceiling."

Chuy glared at Maria for several more moments before finally loosening his grip and rising.

As she hesitantly followed, Maria sensed a depth of rage in Chuy she had never experienced before, and it scared her. His anger was legendary, of course, but in this case Maria felt something more, something much more.

Maria walked a few steps, then abruptly turned and crossed her arms. "You were gonna hit me," she challenged. "Weren't you?"

"Yes, damn you," he said, "but…"

"It's enough that you wanted to," she sighed, tearing up.

Chuy stared at the floor. "How'd she die?"

"Tio shot her at the clinic as she was trying to escape."

When he straightened, it seemed as if his powerful body carried the weight of the world.

Softening, Maria gently touched his arm, "Oh, Chuy, I'm so sorry, but Kat never woke me."

"That's crazy, why would she do such a thing?"

"She loved me. She didn't want to put me in danger, and…and she felt the same about you. I really tried; but there was nothing I could do."

Chuy pulled away, slammed his fist against the wall and turned to leave.

Awakened by his manifest anger, Kathy began to cry in the next room.

"Now you've done it, asshole!" Maria hissed.

"Done what? Who's that?" Chuy demanded.

"My baby," Maria muttered, walking toward the bedroom door.

"*Your* baby? What the hell are you talking about?"

As he entered the semi-darkened room, Chuy instantly realized what Maria had done.

"You can't just keep it. You've gotta know that."

Maria leaned protectively over the crib. "Yes I can!" she shot back. "She's mine—God gave her to me."

"You're fucking crazy," Chuy snapped, turning again to leave.

As she watched him go, Maria suddenly remembered how precious he was to her—how she needed him—now, more than ever.

"Chuy, please...," she called after him, but he was gone.

Chapter 32

*God pours life into death and death into life
without a drop being spilled.*

—Author Unknown

Considering the season, the chapel at Our Lady of Sorrows Church had been a fortuitous selection. Although its gardens, which extended unbroken throughout the adjoining Brackenridge park, were devoid of their normal profusion of color, its towering trees continued to exude strength, peace, and reassuring permanence.

> In Memory of: Katherine Aislin Reed
> Born: March 1, 1980
> Died: September 14, 2007
> Surviving family: None

> At the specific request of the deceased—Katherine Aislin Reed—this service is being conducted in silence. Attendees are encouraged to pause for reflection or prayer; however, no formal presentation will be made.

"Amazing Grace" played softly in the background as the Employee Relations Supervisor paused at the chapel entrance to read the unusual notice. With the words "surviving family" flowing across her consciousness, she was reminded of the uniqueness of this tragedy.

As she entered, the supervisor discretely searched among the various flower arrangements for some indication of a contribution from Southwestern. Her failure, confirmed her initial suspicion that the companies' only acknowledgement of corporate culpability, was to allow a modest extension to the employee's lunch period, "so that all might attend the service." The supervisor was also acutely aware, that, had it not been for preparations initiated—and paid for in advance—by Kat herself, even this modest service might not have taken place.

The supervisor sat for a moment contemplating her personal responsibility in not investigating the rumors regarding Kat, in a more thorough and timely manner. It seems we all failed her, and her baby, she thought, wiping a tear.

Returning from her musing on Kat's demise, the supervisor recognized the picture that had previously adorned Amy Gant's desk. Obviously reflecting a happier time, an exceedingly pregnant Kat smiled back at the observer as if all was well within her world.

Rising, the supervisor placed a rose, whose thorns had been punishing her hands, next to Kat's picture and slowly left the church.

With evening approaching, the intermittent stream of concerned inevitably trailed off into nothingness—leaving Kat in peace.

In time, representatives from the mortuary would arrive to retrieve her mortal remains. The flowers would go to a local nursing home, in accordance with Kat's instructions. Her remains, however, were to be cremated as soon as possible. Not soon enough for Southwestern, of course, long accustomed to quickly burying its mistakes.

As they closed her casket, however, they would undoubtedly miss the small angelic figurine placed within the folds of Kat's shroud, next to her breast.

And so, to the ashes from whence she had come, Kat would finally return.

Chapter 33

Amy's heart soared when she discovered the letter among the pile of mail on her desk. The week had been unbearably stressful since Maria's escape to Bandera. First, there had been the "official" announcement of Kat's death, followed by word of Tio's arrest. Then, a few days later, one of the company lawyers had come around asking questions, claiming he had been assigned to the defense. Amy almost had a coronary over that one, until she realized he had not a clue as to the depth of her relationship with Kat.

The news of Kat's death hit the company hard, especially after it became clear that Tio was somehow involved. As more and more of the graphic details leaked, the usual male-female polarization evaporated. It quickly became obvious to everyone that whatever the "legal" outcome, Tio's relationship with Southwestern was rapidly drawing to a close.

Understandably then, it was with trembling hands that Amy tore open Maria's letter. It began simply...

"Hey Amy,

Just a quick note to let you know that Kathy (yes, I've decided to call her Kathy) and I are home safe and sound—thank goodness.

I'm sorry I haven't written sooner, but I felt it best we get some protection around us first...just in case. Anyway, thanks for leaving the phone message about Kat's service. I still can't believe she's gone. I loved her so much, it hurts even to breathe when I think about her. It's like there's a hole in my heart that even Kathy may not be able to fill. Chuy's having trouble dealing with it too. He was here the other day and we had a horrible fight. I tried to explain what happened, but I'm afraid he still thinks I could have done something more. So now, I may have lost him as well.

Before I forget, Mom says to remind you to plan on coming out for Kathy's baptism. I still don't know when that'll be, however, since the Priest is being a butt again. He says the only way he can morally baptize a 'heathen'—he's not buying the story about Kathy being Catholic—is if the baby was in imminent danger of dying. He actually said anybody could do it under those dire circumstances. I really think he's just trying to stay as far away from me as he can. I guess he considers me bad luck. Anyway, I really didn't like the sound of all that, so I insulted him. I know I shouldn't have, especially since we may need him, but he really pissed me off.

Speaking of Kathy, I swear she's gonna be the death of me if she doesn't settle down and start sleeping more. She's so active and interested in everything. She throws a fit every time I put her down—especially at night. She definitely has Kat's temper.

You know, of course, I'm only kidding; she's really such a joy.

I was able to get all the baby clothes and some of her toys from the apartment before we left, but none of the furniture except for her infant seat. Fortunately, my relatives have lots of baby stuff. Thanks to them, Kathy has the cutest little crib, which of course she's never in, and an almost new high chair for when she grows a bit. About the only thing we've had to buy is a ton of formula and diapers. Jesus, this kid's efficient. Sometimes I swear the stuff's coming out the bottom before it even goes in the top.

By the way, Mom's a real trip. She cries every time she picks Kathy up, which thankfully is a lot. I get the feeling she thinks Kathy is *her* gift from God.

I'm worried so many people know we're back in town though. Before long, somebody will tell my relatives in San Antonio, and that's too close for comfort. Speaking of San Antonio, has anyone been around asking questions? I figure it's only a matter of time before the police learn about Kathy and me.

I had hoped to make a midnight trip back to the apartment, but I just have this lingering dread. Besides, even though I still have a key, I haven't paid the rent, so I imagine everything's gone into storage by now.

That's about it. Not much else has changed around here, as if it ever did, except the town finally added a weird inscription to Juan's memorial in the park. Tell me if this doesn't sound strange to you.

'Take care my friend as you pass by; for as you are, so once was I. And in your haste you may not see; as I am now, you soon shall be.'

I can't imagine why they used that old saying, but I guess it's better than nothing.

Well, as I said, this'll be short.

Let me know if you learn anything about 'you know who.'

I'll write later…M"

You're right, Amy thought, folding the letter tightly in her hand. Please don't come back, it's not safe.

"Amy...Amy honey are you there?" the supervisor's voice sliced into her abstraction.

"Yes...Yes I'm here." She leaned closer to the intercom. "I guess I was just somewhere out in space."

Her supervisor chuckled. "Well, when you land, please bring me your latest numbers."

Quickly slipping Maria's letter into her desk, Amy picked up the charts and headed for the elevator, just as the envelope, with its return address, caught her eye. Now that wasn't very smart, she thought, dropping it into the shredder. The less everyone knows about you, the better.

Chapter 34

How quickly a 'woman's right to choose' comes to serve a 'man's right to use.'
—Juli Loesch

The soft click and whirring sound emanating from Tio's stereo awakened him from yet another unsuccessful attempt at obtaining a restful night's sleep. With Selena's powerful voice permeating the semi-darkened room, Tio carefully pushed himself up into a sitting position and tightened the adjustment straps on his back support—a procedure he was growing more accustomed to, and resentful of, each passing day.

Tio rotated his body and slowly lowered his legs over the side of the bed, before grasping the recently acquired walker and pulling himself to his feet. The nausea that frequently accompanied this daily regimen subsided quickly. Hesitantly moving toward the bathroom, he inadvertently entered a shaft of sunlight streaming through a gap in his carelessly drawn shades. As the intense beam seared into his wounded eye, he shrank back, as if the illumination revealed a fearful pestilence brewing within his soul.

Tio entered the bathroom, and slowly adjusted the electronic dimmer until he recognized the ghostly specter staring back at him from within the mirror. The recognition was not comforting. Gone was the almost God-like visage he once admired at length. Nature's perfection had now been replaced by an ugly, imperfectly healed laceration angling up from his chin, across an uneven lip, and finally passing through his right eye, whose once crystal-clear orb lay shattered beyond redemption. Shattered as well was any fantasy he might have entertained about his future at Southwestern.

"Maria...Maria's ruined my life," he grumbled. "I swear she'll pay dearly for what she's done."

If there was anything left in Tio's life to be thankful for, it was that at least he was home. He still did not fully understand the fortuitous nature of his being granted bail, something his lawyer had initially assured him would *not* happen. Apparently, things were going on in the background, things that were to his advantage, of which he was not yet aware. Tio made a mental note to listen more closely to his lawyer during their meeting that afternoon.

Tio gingerly opened the door on the third ring, which was quite an improvement over his performance of only the previous day.

As the lawyer entered, his demeanor made it obvious he disliked making house calls, necessary or not.

For his part, it was clear Tio could not care less what the lawyer liked, or disliked.

True to form, the lawyer started the meeting by asking Tio if he had any questions.

"Just one." Tio settled into an easy chair. "Tell me again why I'm not in jail."

"Well," the lawyer began, "after the autopsy report was released, the D.A. reduced your charges to aggravated assault and introducing a gun into an abortion clinic."

"That's good, right?" Tio asked.

"Good, but not good enough. You're still looking at significant jail time if things don't go our way."

"What do you mean…'go our way'?"

"We'll get to that in a moment. Any more questions?"

"Why were the charges reduced?"

"That, my friend, is one of the more interesting points I've discovered. According to the Medical Examiner, Katherine Reed—the deceased—died from a botched abortion and not from any direct action of yours."

"You're kidding!"

"Nope, I'm serious as sin. In fact, it appears Ms. Reed actually authorized the procedure that ultimately led to her death."

"That's bullshit, why would she do such a thing?"

"Well, it seems she was more interested in the safe delivery of her baby than in her own life—an interesting concept, wouldn't you agree? Anyway—"

"Wait a minute." Tio broke in. "What baby? She was there for an abortion, not a delivery. Where's the baby?"

"That's what I was getting to when you interrupted me. It seems someone at the clinic, not a staff member mind you, took the baby and hasn't been heard from since."

"Do they know who it was…the person who took the baby?"

The lawyer rummaged through his notes. "Someone named, Maria-something-or-other."

"Vargas," Tio added bitterly.

"That's right, Maria Vargas. Don't tell me you know her."

"Unfortunately, yes. Do they have any idea where she might be?"

"Not a clue as far as I can tell. Do you have any idea how many Maria Vargases there are in San Antonio, not to mention all the outlying communities?"

"You might try talking to Amy Gant at Southwestern; I understand she and Kat were tight. I'll bet she knows where Maria is."

"I already tried that and got nowhere. In fact, the whole company seems pretty unimpressed with my defending you, considering the rumors."

"Fuck'em all," Tio scoffed.

"From what I've heard, you've been doing just that for years."

"Very funny."

"Sorry. Unfortunately, there's only so much we can do without finding Maria. Any other ideas?"

"No, just Amy. You really didn't get anything outa her?"

"Nothing much. In fact, she got downright hostile when I mentioned Maria."

"I thought she might."

The lawyer paused a moment, then…"What the hell's going on, Tio?"

"What do you mean?"

"Well, for one thing, what's all this shit with everyone—including you—playing 'I've got a secret'?"

"It's pretty obvious they're covering for her."

"All of them?" the lawyer asked. "Now, why do you suppose they'd do that?"

"Maybe you should ask Maria. That is, if you ever find her."

The lawyer smiled confidently. "Oh, we'll find her all right."

Yeah, Tio thought smugly, but not before I do. After several moments of silence, he continued. "What about the apartment?"

"I went out there, but everything's gone. Somebody didn't waste any time hauling it all away."

"Another dead end?"

"Not exactly. I do have a copy of the police report."

"Anything interesting?" Tio asked.

"Well, they found the apartment 'disrupted,' but not exactly burglarized. It looked like someone had gone through the place in a big hurry, but apparently didn't take anything of value."

"Sounds like Maria again."

"What would she want that was so important?" the lawyer asked.

"You mentioned a baby. Maybe she picked up some baby things."

The lawyer flipped through the report. "Makes sense I guess, but something else, doesn't."

"What's that?"

"It seems Ms. Reed was loaded. The police found a bunch of financial statements relating to some trusts she'd inherited."

"How's that strange?" Tio asked.

"Well, for one thing, our little Maria's listed as the principle beneficiary, which means her name's all over the stuff and yet she leaves it in the apartment? If she were running, why would she make it so easy for the police to identify her? Unless, of course, she wasn't running from the police at all."

"So, what do you make of it?"

"Actually, it looks pretty bad for Maria."

"Bad?" Tio bent to adjust his back support. "How?"

"It could be argued that the baby and trust funds were more of a motivation for Maria to want Ms. Reed dead than for you. What if she was manipulating the deceased? What if she forcibly prevented Ms. Reed from getting an abortion, and even moved in with her to ensure she made it to term? Under that scenario, you could probably come out looking like some kind of hero. We could show you were actually trying to help the deceased obtain the abortion she so desperately wanted, and that she'd given you her gun so you could protect her from Maria. I imagine we can also show that if it hadn't been for Maria's vicious attack, causing the gun to accidentally go off, Ms. Reed might still be with us."

"That could be a hard sell, considering the witnesses."

"What witnesses? It seems the medical staff didn't actually *see* you shoot anyone. In fact, they're prepared to state Maria bragged about 'kicking your ass,' I believe that's how she put it, before taking the baby."

"Which means?"

"It means Maria could easily have gotten access to the gun. You see, with a little luck you could be guilty of nothing more than being a convenient scapegoat."

"You really think a jury would buy all that?"

"They don't have to buy it all, just enough to establish a reasonable doubt in their collective mind that you're guilty—or at least not provably so."

"That's it? That's your great strategy for saving my ass?"

"Only if necessary. Initially I think we should just play it by ear and see how it goes."

"You don't happen to have any other plans do you," Tio rasped, "just in case?"

"Nope, that's it. Oh, there is one problem, a big one. In order to do this right, we really need to get Maria on the stand. Not only do we have to demonstrate how and why she would do what we contend, but we also have to create some doubt about you. Realistically, the only way that can be done, is to drag Maria into court and eviscerate her."

"I take it then that the next step is to find Maria."

"You got it," the lawyer said, "and I can use all the help I can get."

Tio grinned. "I'll see what I can do."

Chapter 35

Anger and revenge, the twin horsemen of hate, relentlessly depleted Tio's endurance. Indeed, as he collapsed into Amy's chair and closed his eyes, Tio's remaining strength had finally deserted him. From the car, where each pedal-tap and wheel-turn elicited a searing response from his back, to the dark passage down a seemingly endless hall, the painful journey from his apartment to Amy's cube had taken all the stamina he could enlist.

Tio struggled to clear his mind as waves of nausea swept over him. It had been three years, maybe four, since he had visited Amy each morning at her desk. That was a strangely magical time for Tio, and, he was sure for Amy as well. It had also been the first time, and the last, that Tio seriously contemplated a monogamous future. Fortunately, as Amy's friends would later point out, the affair did not last. Over time, the always-edgy relationship changed. Amy would call…Tio would evade. Amy would cry…Tio would get angry. And so it went, until little was left of the passion which once filled Amy's heart. Finally, there was the baby and the abortion. Now, as Tio perused the top of her desk, their love-hate metamorphosis was finally complete.

As he reached for her Southwestern telephone log, Tio had little hope of finding what he sought. Amy had always been careful to keep her personal life out of company records, so it was not too surprising when an entry for Maria was absent from the list.

Tio pushed himself away from the desk. Retrieving a tool from his pocket, he commenced to pick the center lock, which yielded after several awkward attempts. He pulled the drawer out a few inches, reached down, and opened the now unlocked file at his right knee. A few minutes later, finding nothing of value, he slammed the file shut again with his foot.

Come on Amy, he thought, sliding the desk drawer out as far as it would go. You must have left me something!

Tio smiled, as rummaging through the contents, he recognized Amy's address book.

Now we're getting somewhere, he thought, thumbing through the pages.

Amy's entire history was discernable from the contents of her directory. There were entries for friends; old and new, familiar faces, forgotten places, dreams—and of course, Tio, but not Maria. Unnerved at discovering his address still in her record, Tio swore under his breath and tossed the book back into the drawer.

Tired and depressed from his unproductive search, Tio rose to leave just as a tightly folded object fell to the floor.

Tio could hardly believe his luck as he retrieved the letter and quickly scanned its contents. It had to be from Maria. Elated at what he had found, Tio headed for the relative privacy of his office.

Settling back in his chair, Tio removed the letter from his pocket and read it once again. Although there was no specific reference as to Maria's exact whereabouts, he felt certain there was a valuable clue in the vaguely familiar passage…"Take care my friend as you pass by; for as you are, so once was I."

Tio lowered his head in concentration and tried to remember. "I know I've heard that somewhere before, but where?"

Tio ignored the pain in his back as he leaned forward and quickly entered the phrase into his computer. After a few seconds, the display began listing match after match. Because the Internet contained literally hundreds of millions of documents, he knew it could potentially generate countless possibilities to check. Indeed, after spending several minutes scanning through the results, Tio wondered if he might have to refine his search—just as one of the entries caught his eye.

"'The Bandera Tragedy.' Of course…the hanging tree." A smile crossed Tio's disfigured lips. "So Bandera's where our little Maria's been hiding."

Satisfied that he had found what he needed, Tio wasted no more time leaving Southwestern, using the same arduous route by which he had come.

Chapter 36

"Good morning y'all," Amy called as she arrived at her desk later that morning.

Mentally recording each coworker's response, Amy tended the threads within their social fabric. She had always enjoyed these first few moments at work, although she was not quite sure why.

I guess it's much like a precious heirloom, she thought, each worn bit of cloth noticed, each broken strand, missed.

After sitting for a moment changing from walking shoes to heels, Amy stood and leaned over her desk to discuss the latest calamity reports. As she did, however, she felt her center drawer move.

Intrigued by this highly unusual event, Amy bent down and hesitantly pulled on the drawer. When it slid open, her casual interest abruptly changed to a sense of impending doom.

After quickly checking the drawer's contents, Amy was relieved to find that nothing appeared to be missing.

Her concern was understandable, for along with her personal possessions, sensitive company documents were also potentially at risk.

"Hey, my desk's unlocked," she announced, feeling a bit sheepish. "Have you guys seen anyone messing around my cube?"

"Just maintenance emptying the trash. Why, is anything missing?"

"Doesn't look like it," Amy responded. "At least my checkbook and mad money are both still here."

"Maybe you just forgot to lock it when you left last night."

"It's possible I guess, but I could swear…"

"Well, since nothing's missing, don't call security. Those bastards will just shit in your personnel file for leaving the drawer unlocked."

Oh, now that's tacky, Amy thought, reaching for her morning mail.

Despite her best efforts to stay busy throughout the day, Amy kept revisiting the bizarre event in her mind. Embarrassment over leaving the drawer unlocked caused most of her distress, but there was also an element of foreboding, that she just could not shake.

Regardless, after securely locking the drawer when she left for the evening, Amy finally put her tattered emotions to rest. In fact, as she settled onto her couch with a goblet of after-dinner Merlot, the events of her day infringed far less upon her reverie than those of the previous week.

It *had* been a horrendous week, she thought. First the unsettling scene with Tio's lawyer over poor Kat, and then the letter from Maria…

As the memory of Maria's letter traversed her mind, Amy felt a strange tingle deep within the pit of her stomach, which, halfway through her next thought, erupted into her consciousness like a fourth of July fireworks display.

Her letter, where's Maria's letter?

Although her body froze in time, Amy's mind raced through implications of the question.

"Dear God!" she cried, grabbing her bag off the floor and dumping its contents on the bar. "It's just got to be here."

Shaken at not finding the letter, Amy scooped everything back into her bag and headed for the door. Racing across town, she tried to remember where she might have put it. Tell me I didn't just leave the letter out on my desk, she thought. God, I couldn't have been *that* stupid, could I?

A gentle rain began falling; pelting the outside windows along the corridor as Amy rushed toward her cube. Arriving out of breath, she dropped her bag onto the floor and flipped on the overhead light. Quickly slipping to her knees, she inserted her key into the center drawer, then paused—fresh scratches around the lock catching her eye.

Amy ran her fingers over the marred surface. Why didn't I see these before? She wondered.

After taking but a moment to check the contents of her desk, Amy finally faced the nightmare that had stalked her all evening long.

"Damn!" she grumbled in disgust. "Damn, Damn, Damn!"

Throughout her search, she had hoped to evade the only plausible explanation for the missing letter and the fresh scratches. *Tio, it had to be Tio!*

Amy realized she had not a moment to loose, so, quickly grabbing the phone, she dialed Maria's number.

Come on...come on Maria, pick up.

After what seemed like an eternity, she heard Maria's sleepy voice across the void.

"Maria? Oh thank God!" she gasped. "Sweetie, I think we've got big trouble."

Chapter 37

Biology is the least of what makes a mother.
—Oprah Winfrey

Alarmed by the lateness of the call, Maria listened intently before dropping the phone and racing toward Kathy's room. Entering the darkened nursery, she frantically ran her hands over the empty sheet, until…

"You little stinker," she scolded, feeling Kathy's tiny foot sticking out from under her quilt. "Don't scare Mommy like that."

Her sleep disturbed, Kathy began to fuss.

"I'm sorry, Baby," Maria said, quickly lifting her out of the crib, "but we have to go."

Maria held Kathy close and headed for the living room to get her keys and purse. Upon arriving, however, she immediately froze as a large shadow swept across her front window in the moonlight.

Wind gusts had been building all day as a storm approached out of the south. Hesitantly moving toward the door, Maria prayed the shadow was just another tree limb blowing in the wind. After placing her palm against the surface, however, she immediately pulled back, when she heard something metallic being inserted into the lock and the door being forced against its frame. Slowly at first, then with increasing urgency, Maria backed away. As she felt the far wall against her body, she turned and ran barefoot through the kitchen and out across the yard. Slipping into shadows along the fence, Maria winced when she heard the heavy screen door slam shut behind her.

Damn, she thought, I should've been more careful.

After a tense moment listening for a sound of pursuit, Maria stepped through the gate and hurried up the alley.

Tio paused at the sound of the slamming door. Suspecting the worst, he turned and jumped from the porch, only to collapse painfully onto the grass.

"I'm *really* gonna enjoy killing that bitch," he groaned, rising slowly and staggering toward his car.

Tio knew he would never overtake Maria on foot. His only chance was to anticipate her next move. The question remained of course, as to just *what* her next move might be. Maria could head for the safety of a relative's home. If that were the case, he knew his plans would fail. After a moment, however, he realized another possibility. Tio smiled, placed the car in gear and slowly drove away.

Maria had walked to Chuy's house on numerous occasions as a child. Then, possibly because she always enjoyed the adventure, the path seemed smoother to her bare, but wellcalloused feet.

Time and Mother Nature had changed all that. Now each step reminded her, the child was a woman, with a woman's soft feet.

Although she hurried as best she could over the uneven terrain, a pursuing wind still overtook her, surrounding them in clouds of swirling dust.

Finally, after what seemed like an eternity, Maria saw the faint outline of Chuy's house looming out of the darkness.

Rain began to fall as she hurried up the steps and banged on the door. Desperate, Maria peered through the front window, looking for some indication Chuy might be home. Unfortunately, the house seemed deserted except for a small light coming from somewhere off the hall. As the wind's intensity increased, Maria wrapped the quilt tighter around Kathy and descended the front steps. Struggling through wind-whipped shrubs to the side yard, she discovered Chuy's car missing. "Damn it, Chuy! Where are you?"

Returning to the porch, she stood for a moment staring in dread at the storm. It was clear; the open veranda would not protect them long. Maria realized the church might be her only refuge. In the hope that Chuy would come for them; she wrapped her crucifix around the doorknob as a sign of her distress, then descended the familiar old steps once again.

Maria's delicate gown pressed against her legs as she struggled into the wind. Kathy, frightened by the turmoil, began to cry, disturbing a succession of neighborhood dogs. Maria knew the incessant barking would eventually bring unwanted attention, possibly from Tio. She had to do something if they were to have any chance of reaching the church. Quickly unbuttoning her top, she guided Kathy's mouth to her breast.

Even without milk, the strange sensation was overpowering. Not since her Juan's arms, had Maria felt such intense intimacy. Each expression of Kathy's need seemed to translate into a shaft of iced-lightning pulsing through her. Were it not for the approaching storm, she might never have taken another step. Nevertheless, the storm *was* approaching, and so, she continued on.

Arriving at the church, Maria once again slipped into the shadows. By doing so, she hoped to see Chuy's lights as he came for them—*if* he came for them—but also to evade Tio. Unfortunately, Heaven refused to cooperate. The torrential rain and relentless wind enveloping them, forced Maria to change her plans. With one last desperate glance over her shoulder, she whispered a short prayer and entered the church.

The contrast between the violence of the storm without, and the serenity of the church within, struck Maria. As she paused at the entrance, she felt as if transported into another world. Although it had been only a few days since attending Mass in this very room, her mind seemed to take her further back…back to her time of grace, back to her time with God.

Little had changed in the intervening months. There was still the majesty: the flickering candles, the statues, the cross…and Christ. There were still rows of pews running left and right, as if to illustrate the choice between good and evil. Finally, there were the pillars, rising toward Heaven at one end, descending toward Hell at the other. As Maria waited, lost somewhere along the path between hope and hopelessness, a shadow reached to remove the patch over its damaged eye.

Maria must see what she has done, Tio thought; and understand why she will die.

Maria was afraid.

Alone with Kathy in her arms, she felt no comforting touch, saw no guiding light, heard no calming voice. In fact, her emotions were much the same as the first time she had confronted God with her sins, and was forgiven—or so she had thought at the time. With the storm's full fury settling in above them, however, Maria realized her water had yet to be turned into wine.

"Chuy, where are you?" she groaned, as precious minutes slipped by. She was sure Tio was still out there…searching, and it was only a matter of time before he found them.

"Imminent danger…anyone can do it." The words had smoldered in the back of her mind since Amy's call.

What if Kathy died before being baptized? Would God even acknowledge her? Would Heaven accept her?

Maria decided she could wait no longer. Holding Kathy close, she whispered, "I think it's time we introduced you to God."

It had taken so long for Maria to arrive that Tio had almost given up hope. However, with the sound of her entrance, he put aside any concern she might somehow escape his wrath. Indeed, at any moment, Chuy might have come or the storm might have passed and she might have gone.

Instead, Maria felt a crushing blow, as if a shaft of lightning had somehow violated the sanctuary, pierced her side, and was driving her to her knees.

Maria screamed...

Gasping for breath, she instinctively reached out to grab the side of a pew as she fell.

With her mind struggling to understand what was happening, Maria sensed a presence kneeling beside her, and felt the cold steel of a gun placed against her temple.

"Tio!" she gasped.

He brushed her ear with his lips. "You don't feel so tough now, do you?"

Maria gently lowered Kathy to the floor, then, turning to face Tio, hissed, "Go to Hell!"

Livid at her continued defiance, Tio slapped her hard, slamming her to the floor, splitting her lip.

Maria pulled herself up against the pew, her breath coming in short, painful gasps. "Please," she pleaded, as he once again pressed the gun against her head, "just don't hurt my baby!"

He watched the terror of her mistake spill into her eyes. *Finally, he knew...* knew how to pierce her heart.

A smile of cruel satisfaction crossed his lips as he turned the gun toward Kathy. Before his finger closed over the trigger, however, a bolt of lightning exploded above them. Painful, multi-hued shards of light streamed into Tio's unprotected eye, transforming reality within his sight. For the briefest moment, he saw...

Then it was over.

Once again, Maria knelt beside him, reaching to protect her baby. Once again, her breathing was little more than a wheeze. Once again, she was dying.

"God!" Tio raised a hand to his forehead. "What've I done?"

After standing for a moment, alone in his despair, Tio placed the gun on an adjacent pew and turned toward the exit.

Maria watched him go. Slowly lowering her head, she closed her eyes and pleaded with her God, "End this ...please!"

The rain had finally stopped. Stepping through the doorway, Tio felt the cool night breeze envelope him. As he raised his eyes to drink deeply of its cleansing brew, an iron grip closed around his throat.

Slammed back against the wall, he struggled in vain until, faint from lack of air; he barely noticed the blade enter his groin.

Chapter 38

The purpose of life is a life of purpose.
—Robert Byrne

The aromal perfume of desert flowers wafting on the morning breeze awakened Tio. At the sound of distant thunder, he lazily turned his head to watch the remnants of last evening's storms move off to the north. Glancing back at the eternal struggle between fading stars and the rising sun, he pondered for a moment the beauty of the dawn…but only for a moment.

Unwillingly pulled from the intoxication of his dream, Tio tried to rise, but a paralyzing spike forced him back. Distracted by the numbing residue of pain washing through his groin, he failed to notice a rapid movement near the corner of his eye—the movement of an ant!

Possibly the smell of coagulating blood running down his legs first attracted the ants, or maybe a lone…Well, it really did not matter.

As the full gravity of his plight struck him, Tio convulsed in a spasm of all-consuming panic. Straining against his bindings, he mixed the blood of his wrists with the sweaty stench of fear streaming from his body, to no avail.

He labored against the ants for as long as he could, but their relentless attack was chillingly efficient. Tio tried to flick, or blink them off his eyes, but they merely rode the lids, taking small slices as they went. Eventually, he could do little else but to close his eyes and wait, until the chemical-rich flow of tears led the ants to the muscles holding them shut. Once severed, the lids were slowly peeled back, exposing his twin orbs to the merciless assault of the midday sun—and to the ants.

Tio's mind watched in horror as they systematically sliced through and removed his corneas and the gelatinous material beyond. No longer protected, his exposed optic nerves became a matrix of misery leading inward toward eternal darkness.

Long before the sun ascended to its throne, Tio's other senses were taken from him as well. Swarms of ants entered his ears and quickly breached the thin membranes providing sound and a barrier to the brain. His nose and throat also fell victim to the teaming hordes harvesting his body. Having lost spatial awareness, Tio vomited. Immediately, however, the rich mixture of bile and blood became a seething river of death as they followed it back down deep within his body.

Distractions of the outside world stripped away, Tio's mind concentrated on the assault from within. Each centimeter traversed, each centimeter remaining in their relentless quest, was calculated in exquisite detail. Eventually, he sensed more than felt their arrival within his brain. Accepting the inevitability of its demise, Tio's mind went into overdrive distributing the chemicals of death. In a blinding flash of drug-induced awareness, he glimpsed the entirety of his wasted life—and ceased to be.

They found what was left of Tio, in the early evening. The South Texas sun, having relentlessly baked the desert sands for yet another day, was finally settling into the horizon as the patrol twisted through the final leg of its daily sweep along the border.

It was not unusual to find unfortunates. There were always the immigrants, clamoring to cross a river of water, only to die of thirst on the other side. Occasionally, there were remnants of drug deals gone bad, deals where the wages of sin included a bullet in the head. But this one was different, more personal. This one was family.

Being staked out and left to God's mercy was harsh enough, but at least you had a chance. In this case, as boot tracks through the anthill clearly revealed, little was left to God.

There would be a report, of course, followed by the usual forensics to determine who to bury and who to burden, as if it really mattered. In cases like this, everyone needing to know, probably already did.

After standing for a long moment counting their blessings, the officers turned and walked slowly back to their Jeep.

Chapter 39

Here is the test to find out whether your mission on earth is finished: If you're alive, it isn't.

—Richard Bach

Maria awakened...

"Not you again," she groaned, recognizing her aunt Virginia. "Where's Kathy?"

"Nice to see you too, dear."

"Where's...Kathy?" Maria demanded.

"She's fine. She's with your Mom."

Maria tried to sit up. "I don't feel so good. How bad is it?"

"Well, you've got a nasty bullet hole in your side, a cracked rib, and your teeth are loose again. Other than that, you're fine."

"Crap!"

"Seriously, if you don't stop this shit, you're gonna get yourself killed."

Maria touched the crucifix, which had mysteriously returned to her. "Don't worry, it's over."

"How do you know?"

Maria attempted a smile. "God told me."
"Here we go with the God stuff again."
"No, I mean it this time—it's over!"

As the bus pulled out of the station and headed east toward San Antonio, Maria thought back to what the kindly old woman had whispered to her a few moments before. What was it she'd said? Something about God's love, children, and forgiveness. With the old woman's words lying softly on her mind, Maria held her Kathy…her dream, closed her eyes and slept.

Epilogue

"What now?" Amy growled, as the insistent banging intensified.

She reached across her keyboard, launched the security-cam on her PC and scrolled the view. As she focused on the obviously irritated specter at her door, Amy marveled once again at Kathy's similarity to her mother, Kat. There was the same winsome form, topped by a rambling mop of soft auburn hair, the same captivating eyes. Unique to Kathy, however, was her explosive personality, now displayed in angry abundance.

Poor Maria, Amy thought, as she rose and switched off the display. She never had a chance of taming that shrew.

"She *lied* to me!" Kathy said, bursting through the door.

"Excuse me?"

"She lied to me, and I'll bet you were in on it from the start."

"Kathy, what're you talking about? Where's your mother?"

"She's not my mother, and you know it!"

"Damn," Amy sighed. "I think I'd better sit down for this one."

"Dandy idea," Kathy said, as she stomped into the kitchen and yanked open the refrigerator.

"Just make yourself at home, dear," Amy called after her.

Ignoring the dig, Kathy plopped onto the couch and twisted the cap off her Evian. "Auntie, it's time to come to Jesus."

Amy dodged. "What makes you think I'd know anything?"

Kathy raised a skeptical eyebrow. Her stare bore deep into Amy as she continued. "Don't pull that innocent crap with me; you know perfectly well what I'm talking about. You're guilty as sin, just like this…this Maria person."

"This…Maria…person," Amy repeated. "I assume that would be your mother?"

"Did you really think I wouldn't find out? What'd you do, babynap me or something?"

"No, we didn't 'babynap you or something.'"

"Well it sure looks like it. It's obvious; Maria's not my real mother."

A chill raced down Amy's spine. "Who've you been talking to?"

"Nobody; I figured it all out myself."

"Very clever I guess," Amy scoffed, "but it seems like much ado about nothing."

"Nothing huh? Look at my green eyes; they had to come from somewhere…Duh!"

"So that's what all this is about? Your green eyes?"

"You know Maria's are brown. Besides, I discovered something very interesting in her lingerie drawer this morning."

"And just what were you doing in her lingerie drawer, young lady?"

"I needed some panties, all mine were gross."

"You might try washing them."

"I do...sometimes. Anyway, there was this album with lovey-dovey photos of her and some Latino guy."

"What's special about that? You're Latina."

"Part...part Latina! The dude in the pictures had brown eyes!"

"I don't understand..."

"There's like, only one chance in a gazillion a brown-eyed couple can make a green-eyed baby."

Amy grimaced. "Have you considered that maybe you're just really special?"

Once again raising an eyebrow, Kathy fired another scorcher.

Amy stood, and then walked to the window as if searching for some avenue of escape. Finding none, she turned.

"What difference does it make?" she finally relented. "Maria's always been there for you...she's probably the reason you were even born."

"What's that supposed to mean?"

"It means, 'Miss-behavior,' that when she rescued your happy ass, you were a heartbeat away from being thrown into a stainless steel garbage can."

"You mean...an abortion? You expect me to believe that, after all this?"

"Go ask her yourself. Ask her about that scar below her left breast."

"So my real mother…didn't want me?"

"No, Baby, she loved you. She died, that you might live."

"What are you talking about? Who *are* you people? And just who…who the *hell* am I?"

"We'll get to that in a moment, but first, we need to call your mother and let her know you're safe."

"She's…not…my…MOTHER!"

It was an uncomfortable time for Kathy, as they talked and waited for Maria to arrive. Time enough for her to feel the pain and cry the tears, but not enough to evade the truth. The girl-to-woman metamorphosis thus began for Kathy, just as it had for Maria, many years before. Never again would she careen through life, blind to the consequences of her actions, indifferent to the beat of her heart.

Kathy sighed as Maria's familiar footsteps echoed on the stairs. What was her name? My real mother I mean."

"'Katherine,' but she went by 'Kat.'"

"I was sorta named after her then." Kathy paused; her words were more an answer than a question. "I don't know what to say."

"Don't say anything; just go do something important with your life. You owe it to her…and to God."

The End

Printed in the United States
204411BV00001B/1-105/P